CW00407809

THE BILLIONAIRE'S PREGNANT FLING

JAMESON BROTHERS BOOK TWO

LESLIE NORTH

CONTENTS

JAMESON BROTHERS

The Billionaire's Ex-Wife

The Billionaire's Pregnant Fling

The Billionaire's Sexy Rival

The Billionaire's Pregnant Fling

USA TODAY BESTSELLING AUTHOR

LESLIE NORTH

BLURB

This billionaire playboy has turned over a new leaf—just in time to become a new dad.

Eddie Jameson has held the title of black sheep in the Jameson family for years. Creative, cocky and carefree, Eddie had a reputation for being the life of the party and a pain in the ass when it comes to following procedure. However, back in the flagship branch of the Jameson Agency, Eddie is proving himself to be a new man—someone worthy of his family's' respect.

Margot Dale is the daughter of one of Jameson Agency's most lucrative clients and the girl Eddie has been after for years. New leaf or not, he wants her—and how much harm could bringing the old Eddie back for one night do? When Margot and Eddie meet unexpectedly at a party, sparks fly and a childhood attraction rapidly becomes an adult sexcapade.

Now Eddie's role in the company, and in his family, is on the line. Margot is pregnant and for the first time in her life, unsure of how to handle a situation. The one thing Margot and Eddie know they have is a connection—one that strengthens each other and sets off fireworks between the sheets. But they'll need to decide if love and marriage are really coming with their baby carriage.

MAILING LIST

Thank you for purchasing 'The Billionaire's Pregnant Fling'
(Jameson Brothers Book Two)

Get SIX full-length novellas by USA Today best-selling author Leslie North for FREE! Over 548 pages of best-selling romance with a combined 1091 FIVE STAR REVIEWS!

Sign-up to her mailing list and get your FREE books at:
http://leslienorthbooks.com/sign-up-for-free-books

ABOUT LESLIE

Leslie North is the USA Today Bestselling pen name for a critically-acclaimed author of women's contemporary romance and fiction. The anonymity gives her the perfect opportunity to paint with her full artistic palette, especially in the romance and erotic fantasy genres.

To discover more about Leslie North visit:
LeslieNorthBooks.com

Facebook: fb.com/leslienorthbooks

Twitter: @leslienorthbook

Goodreads: Goodreads.com/author/show/1899287.Leslie_North

Bookbub: Bookbub.com/authors/leslie-north

CHAPTER ONE

EDDIE

His one-night stand was coming back to haunt him, and Eddie Jameson had never been more eager for the reunion.

"Jameson?" The haughty venture capitalist attempted to reclaim his attention. "You all right? The punch hitting you a little too hard there?"

Eddie blinked. He had almost forgotten where he was in the New York bar, and who he was talking to...scratch that, he *had* forgotten who he was talking to. "Yeah. Hey, I'll be with you in a minute," he promised the suit in front of him. Any investment he had in their tedious conversation had gone out the window the moment he noticed the familiar vision sitting alone across the room. Eddie moved past the capitalist, passing off his drink in the process. The other man clearly didn't approve of being treated like a waiter, but Eddie couldn't have cared less. His focus was elsewhere.

It was Margot Daley sitting at the bar. Eddie had known her

since childhood. She was one of his oldest and dearest friends—and the beautiful woman who *also* happened to be his most memorable recent hookup. It had been a slow burn between the two of them, spanning a decade at least; even now, seeing her like this, he couldn't help but mentally replay every thrust and arch and sweet purr of pleasure their union had elicited. Margot was his oldest friend, and his newest lover; it made for an unforgettable combination.

Even if he had never seen her naked before, Eddie would have noticed her now. She bloomed like a rare night flower in a field of interchangeable daisies. Her black cocktail dress stood out starkly against the spring pastels; where other skirts flowed breezily around bare, athletic legs, Margot's skin-tight selection hugged her every curve as intimately as the gaze of a hopeful lover. Every subtle shift of her legs might as well have broadcast itself at a *ten* on the room's male-only frequency.

God, she was gorgeous. Athletic as hell, and as naturally tan as he was from all her time spent outdoors. Even from across the room, Eddie could make out the strikingly dark eyebrows that overshadowed her wide-set, innocent brown eyes; they were both a contrast and a complement to her long, ginger-blond hair.

He was moving toward her before he knew what he was doing. Not that he minded, or even normally ignored, the whims of his body. His hand found her waist almost as soon as she was within reach; it slid along the small of her back in quiet, intimate greeting. Margot started and turned in her stool. Eddie had heard of the deer-in-the-headlights look, but he had never been on the receiving end of it before.

"Eddie!" she exclaimed in astonishment.

"Me," Eddie agreed. "How are you this evening, Margot?"

"What are you doing here?" Her surprise was so profound that Eddie had to momentarily fight to keep his smile fixed in place. She didn't sound exactly *unhappy* to see him, but there was a definite note of disbelief in her voice that made him wonder.

"I have Kyle Moby's fall from grace to thank for my invite tonight," he admitted. "This seat taken?"

Margot shook her head, and Eddie sat down beside her. He let his hand slide from her waist, even though he hated to break contact with her. Her surprise at seeing him had caused him to rethink the familiarities he had been planning.

He conceded privately that it was possible he hadn't been on her mind as much as *she* had been on his, even if it did come as a bit of a blow to his ego. Margot had been almost all he could think about since their searingly-hot night together almost two months ago. She was the distraction he couldn't afford, now that he was finally moving up at the agency and winning his brothers' respect...but she was also the rising addiction he couldn't find it in himself to overcome. Not yet.

There was no denying that Margot looked distracted herself. She had pieced together a simple, stunning outfit, but paid no attention to the season's colors; her golden locks looked teased by the wind rather than any sort of styling apparatus. Eddie would have bet his inheritance that he wasn't the first guy to approach that evening, yet here she was: perched in self-imposed solitude and staring vacantly past the bartender standing sentinel. She didn't even have a drink in front of her.

Something had to be done.

"Kyle Moby? Of Mobius Mobile?" Margot inquired. "I hadn't heard anything. What happened?"

"They dropped him from the Thirty Under Thirty," Eddie confided. "But you didn't hear it from me. The new list comes out this month." He glanced around furtively for show, and Margot leaned in a little. "He made a huge spectacle of himself at their last gathering. This is their first event since Kyle got the boot."

"Well, you've certainly hyped this story enough," Margot said with mock reproof. "Typical of a Jameson."

Eddie preened at the compliment. "What are you drinking? Never mind. I've got it." He signaled to the watching bartender. "Whiskey on the rocks for me, and a whiskey water for my gorgeous friend here. Man, does that guy hover or what? Anyway, back to my story...so Kyle shows up to this party already *completely* black-out drunk, and everyone's pretending like they don't even notice when he can barely pile out of the back of the limousine without three more dudes assisting him. They manage to get him up to the rooftop without incident. My best guess it was his friends' intention to leave him passed out on the sofa, but the sofa they chose happened to be outside the suite...and right beside the pool."

Margot groaned and shook her head. If she thought she already knew where this was going, then she was in for a treat. Eddie settled into his stool and raised his hands as if they were necessary to measure the full scope of Kyle's fuck-up.

"So drunk asshole. Pool. Total lack of supervision. Kyle wakes up a half hour later and immediately unzips."

4

"No." Margot's interjection couldn't stop the train now that it had already left the station.

"Because he's got to take a leak, right? Dude's been drinking since he woke up that morning." Eddie chuckled. "So he starts pissing in the pool. And Phillip Hedlund—Number Twenty-Nine, the guy whose pool it is—comes out and sees this, and he *freaks.* Shoves Kyle into the pool face-first with his pants still around his ankles."

Margot groaned and dropped her forehead into her hand.

Eddie leaned in. "But as we've established already, Kyle's had a *lot* to drink. By now a crowd's gathered, and everyone's watching to see what he'll do next. He manages to get out of the water on his own—pants *still* around his ankles—but Phillip won't stop hollering about his pool. So what does Kyle do? He doesn't want to wear out his welcome any more than he already has. He stumbles over to the edge of the roof, and *pukes* right over the side...only there's another party going on down below. A bachelorette party."

Margot made a choking noise.

"And the girls just start *screaming.*" Eddie waved his hands wildly around his head as if fending off an unexpected shower. It was easy to draw inspiration from Margot's growing grimace of agony. "Suffice it to say, they booted Kyle from the party...and from the top Thirty Under Thirty, which means more room for me. He turns thirty-one next week, anyway." Eddie laughed at the anticlimactic conclusion, and Margot just shook her head in utter disbelief. She had managed to remain mostly disgusted throughout his salacious yarn, but he could tell from the way her eyes glimmered that she was holding back her mirth. *Why* was another story, and one he intended to unravel for himself. He edged his shoulders in a little closer and nudged her. "Anyway, what's new with you? I haven't heard from you since…"

"Since." She echoed the word as if it was more than just an agreement, but a punctuation on what he had been about to say. Her seeming reluctance to bring up the other night didn't faze Eddie. He nudged her again, this time with his knee beneath the bar; after a moment, he felt Margot lean into him slightly. Her body language was less rigid than her conversation, and he took it as an encouraging sign. More than that, he just wanted an excuse to feel the lean line of her thigh pressed against his.

"Look, I'm sorry if I'm the one who dropped the ball," Eddie said. "I've been busy at the agency. And I know you've been busy at the firm. What are you working on these days?"

"Designing new offices, mostly." Margot pulled a new face this time, and Eddie chuckled. She could be endearingly expressive without realizing it, and she looked ten years younger than twenty-eight when they got on a subject she was passionate about. "Those are the only jobs coming in these days, and they're all in affluent neighborhoods. It gets boring after a while: nobody has an original idea or seems willing to take a risk anymore. Everyone just wants to do *exactly* what their competitors are doing."

"They're lucky to have you, then," Eddie said. "They couldn't ask for a more cutting-edge designer. Hell, how many architects still build their own models by hand?" He reached between them to lace her lovely fingers in his under the pretense of giving a demonstration. Margot's mouth quirked even harder at this, but she didn't pull away...even if her eyes told him she knew what he was up to.

"Most people hire out these days," she replied. She let her fingers trace the dips in his knuckles a moment longer, but withdrew the moment the bartender returned. Eddie wasn't discouraged. The entire evening stretched ahead of them like an unspooling velvet ribbon, and he was confident he could guide its course.

"Hmmm. I hate to make a scene, but I think there's been a mistake. *That* looks like water," he mentioned as the bartender set a dubiously translucent glass down in front of Margot. No matter how he turned his head, he couldn't see any sort carbonation rising up from the bottom. He tapped the side of the glass with his finger to be sure, but kept a warm smile in place as he looked between them.

"The lady isn't drinking tonight," the bartender replied curtly. Eddie flexed an eyebrow, but didn't remark on the protective edge he picked up in the other man's voice. It wouldn't be the first time he interrupted another man's attempt to hit on Margot.

"No mistake," Margot volunteered. She plucked her glass up off the table and raised it to Eddie in toast. "I'm not drinking anymore. At least, not for the next nine months."

"Nine months?" Eddie repeated with a laugh. He folded his arms and leaned forward on the bar, already intent on wearing her down. He knew Margot, and she wasn't one to shy from a free round. She must be playing coy tonight because they had an audience. "What's the *lack* of occasion, if I may ask?" He took a long, appreciative sip of his own drink to demonstrate all the fun she was missing.

He ignored the bartender's astonished look. Less easy to ignore was the way Margot's own expressive eyebrows rose in disbelief.

"Are you serious, Eddie? I'm pregnant."

The appreciative sip came back up as a spit-take.

CHAPTER TWO

MARGOT

Margot dodged out of the way as Eddie's drink exited his mouth in a spray. Had they been having any other conversation, she would have found it comical. The bartender's towel came down and mopped the counter as if he'd been expecting as much.

Leave it to Eddie Jameson to not realize the immediate implication of *nine months*. He'd been so busy flirting that he hadn't been able to wrap his head around anything other than what her legs *might* be wrapped around by the end of the evening. The memory of their night together sent an uncontrollable shiver racing through her, but she set it aside—as she often had these past two months—to try and focus on more pressing matters...like the unforeseen consequences of their explosive hookup.

"Yep. Great at biology, but not so good at math, are you?" Margot offered as she took a long pull of water. What she wouldn't give for the burn of that offered whiskey right about now, but she had cut out alcohol the second she found out she was pregnant.

Eddie stared at her like she had just grown a second head...which in a roundabout way, Margot guessed she sort of had. She thought she might find some bittersweet relish, or at least relief, upon breaking the news to Eddie, but neither came easily beneath the weight of his incredulous dark eyes. So she said simply, "I just complimented your prowess, Eddie. You should thank me."

"Thank you," he repeated stiltedly. Then the dreaded question came; no matter how much Margot had prepared herself to face it, she almost lost her nerve knowing what he was about to ask. "Is the baby...?" he began.

"It's yours," she confirmed before he could finish. "We can always test if it would make you feel better."

"I don't feel...I mean...I don't know...*how* I feel," Eddie concluded. He proceeded to drain his drink in a single gulp, looking as if he wanted to order another but couldn't remember how. Margot noticed the bartender watching them raptly; she hoped he was enjoying the unfolding soap opera. Time for the climax.

"I'm keeping it," she stated.

A shot landed in front of Eddie, and he threw it back without looking. He didn't even grimace at what Margot was sure was the astringent sting of a very strong spirit. He surprised her by nodding his head repeatedly in agreement. She sat back to consider the state her bombshell revelation had left him in.

Eddie was, and had probably always been, the single most

attractive man that Margot had ever known. She couldn't remember a time when he *hadn't* been a bronze-skinned Adonis; even back when they were kids, Eddie's love of sailing had meant he rarely spent any time indoors. He'd grown into an outdoorsman boasting a rock-hard musculature to match beneath that expensively-tailored suit...a physique that Margot now had firsthand experience with, she reflected. She had always been content to look before, but never touch. Eddie's father and her own had been old friends, after all, and after Eddie's dramatic affair with the daughter of one of his clients, Margot had under-stood the need to keep things platonic between them.

Or at least, she thought she had.

Their passionate night together wasn't proving easy for her to forget, that was for sure. Baby aside, the memory of sex with Eddie still aroused tingles of anticipation all along her spine as if he was impressed into her bones. Just thinking about what he could do with his *hands* made the insides of her thighs uncom-fortably slick with perspiration; she crossed her legs now to try and push it from her awareness. She could devote more thought to what Eddie could do later when she was alone, and the object of her reflection wasn't sitting directly beside her.

Eddie's gorgeous tan had taken a momentary backseat; now, he looked pale and seasick, a sensation Margot felt certain the accomplished sailor had never experienced before in his life. A stab of guilt hit her. She hadn't wanted to break the news to him this way. She hadn't wanted to break the news to him at *all,* but knew all along that keeping such a massive secret to herself was worse. "Are you all right? You look like you're going to pass out," she mentioned.

"I'm not gonna pass out." The remark was one he would have made when they were kids; an immediate, defensive rebuttal. He ran a hand through his dark brown hair. "You and I need to schedule a meeting. A *real* meeting. That will enable me to get on top of this whole baby thing."

"A meeting?" she repeated incredulously. She wished she didn't find the suggestion amusing—because Eddie clearly did not—but of all the possible reactions she had expected to her baby news, this had to be the last one. She hadn't anticipated his response to be so...*analytical.* She felt equal parts dismayed and impressed by him in that moment. Eddie had managed to turn his own ship around—but it was the Eddie who *didn't* navigate, who went with the ebb and flow of the tide and every mercurial change of the wind, that Margot had grown up adoring. True, his accepting mentality used to drive her crazy, but now that she was older it was something she sought to emulate. Now that she was unexpectedly *pregnant,* she was more determined than ever to go with the flow of things herself. In the past, *she* was the one who had always been the planner: the one who scheduled entire work years in one sitting, the one who inventoried, the one who never had any sort of unexpected fun. She would never admit it, but Eddie was her inspiration to make the change... and she was determined to see it through. She *would* enjoy life the way he did, damn it.

Clearly all that recent time spent shadowing his older brothers at the Jameson Agency had an effect. "Forget the meeting, Eddie. Why don't we set up a focus group to see how well the baby tests?" Her tone wasn't light enough to sound completely teasing, but she wanted to put him at ease. She hated seeing him like this. "But I agree we should...talk about it. Maybe not in a boardroom with a secretary taking minutes, but obviously somewhere that isn't a bar."

"No," Eddie agreed, "you shouldn't be inside *any* bars, Margot."

Her temper flared hot in her chest. "It's not like I was planning on drinking, Eddie. I just needed to be somewhere tonight where there were other people around."

"Right. Other people smoking and vaping and doing God knows what else." His eyes tracked around the room as if he suddenly didn't recognize his surroundings. Margot followed his gaze, but try as she might, she couldn't perceive any of the dangers Eddie seemed privy to. "Do your parents know?"

"They know."

"And they know I'm the father?"

Margot cringed, then nodded slowly. It was a conversation she would rather not relive right here and now. "I'm sorry, Eddie. I wanted to tell you first, but Mom found my pregnancy test, and went and told Dad about it." Margot scowled. "Actually, she told me she went looking for evidence. Turns out she suspected I was pregnant even before I did."

"I should have called," Eddie said adamantly. "When you didn't respond to my texts, I should have called you to make sure you were all right. We've got to make sure you're cutting back on strenuous exercise and eating healthy. Are you set up with a good obstetrician? Have you gone to your first prenatal appointment? You don't have to take me with you if you aren't comfortable; I just want to make sure we're covering all our bases."

Margot blinked and sat back. Now Eddie *really* wasn't

sounding like himself. Where was the affably irresponsible, go-with-the-flow Jameson she had grown up with? "You sound like 'What to Expect When You're Expecting' on steroids," she muttered.

"Exactly why we need to have a meeting," Eddie said. "We need to share information and pool our resources. I think what's probably most important to consider is…"

As he continued to rattle off details, Margot felt herself steadily growing nauseous. Now *she* was the one nodding along without any clear objection to what he was saying. Her skin felt clammy, and she was sure she must look as pale as Eddie had when she broke the news of her pregnancy. How had the tables turned so quickly? Why did *she* suddenly feel like the one who was unprepared?

Wait—was he seriously talking about school districts?

A distracting, buzzing sensation was starting to form behind her ears. Margot recognized it at once, but wanted to hold onto the moment for just a second longer. Of all the times for her to get sick, this was probably the worst she could have chosen. She had finally crossed paths with Eddie and broke the news, and he was being *proactive,* already coming up with solutions to problems she didn't know she had…

But there was no hope for it. Margot's stomach clenched, and a sour taste suddenly filled her mouth. The bartender at least seemed to notice her sudden shift; he pointed her toward a far corner of the room, and she didn't risk nodding to show him she had understood. She stood up quickly, and Eddie cut himself off when the look on her face finally registered with him.

"Margot, are you all right?" His stark brows pulled together in perplexity.

She couldn't shake her head any more than she could nod. There was no doubt in her mind that she was about to throw up. She cupped a hand over her mouth and stumbled back toward the bathrooms, leaving Eddie to trail in her wake.

CHAPTER THREE

EDDIE

Twenty-four hours after taking Margot home, Eddie found himself headed back to the exact same bar. His attendance at the Thirty Under Thirty mixer had mostly been an excuse to scope out the terrain. A month ago he had arranged a client cocktail hour at the bar, and tonight was the night of the event.

He had almost completely forgotten about it until his brother, Sam, reminded him in the final hour.

"Don't you have some sort of reminder system in place?" Samson Jameson was a Roman sculpture of a man, and about as warm on a good day. He followed Eddie out of the backseat of their shared limousine, and paused to confirm instructions with the driver as Eddie gazed up at the plunging, darkened faces of New York City's skyscrapers. Everything about the city was suddenly less familiar to him, more hazardous and sharply-edged. Was this how things started to look when you became a father—even an expecting one?

"I'm not like you," he replied. "I don't have Trinity to help keep my schedule."

"First of all, yes you do. Trinity is always hounding you about appointments," Sam corrected him. "And second of all, *I'm* the one who has to remind Trinity of the work engagements she deems nonessential."

"Great. See? I already have two human fail-safes in place," Eddie concluded.

Sam sighed through his nose and adjusted his tie, which had already been resting perfectly on his chest. "This was a good idea, at any rate: allowing our clients to network and mingle, all while trying out new brands of alcohol and different catering companies. Thanks for setting it up."

"You're welcome." His relationship with Sam had always been formal, almost frigid before, and the thaw that they were now experiencing was still new to him. It made him feel pleased, and awkward, and unworthy, to be on the receiving end of Sam's gratitude. Sam was the middle brother, and the one who had most taken after their father—not only in his work ethic, but in his interpersonal relations. The fact that he had found any reason to thank Eddie at all showed just how far they had come in mending fences.

Eddie's throat clenched at the thought. This was another piece of what he stood to lose if he fucked things up with Margot. He had already betrayed his brothers' trust by sleeping with a client's daughter in the past; what would their reaction be now that he had done it again?

God, but Margot was different. Margot wasn't just the forbidden fruit Eddie had always longed to taste—she was the whole package. Beautiful, intelligent, successful, and, he had previously assumed, immune to his charms. He was the last person who had expected himself to end up between the sheets with her, and it wasn't helping his case that he craved having her again. This baby business should have been occupying the forefront of his brain, but he couldn't shut his primal desire for Margot down, either, no matter how hard he tried. She was all he could think about.

"You should try looking less hungover," Sam advised as they walked through the bar doors together.

After dropping Margot off last night, Eddie may have had a few too many. He didn't acknowledge Sam's reproving remark, but he did turn the wattage up on his smile, and reach up to smooth one eyebrow (and put pressure on a throbbing spot in his temple).

"Eddie!" A client turned away from one of the caterers to greet him. "There he is, the man of the hour! Come and meet my daughter!"

Oh, Jesus, Eddie thought, but kept his Stepford smile fixed in place. He charmed every acquaintance new and old as best he could, and shook hands firmly despite the fact that all this cordial jostling was only making his head pound harder. He noticed Sam raise an eyebrow at him before moving off to make his own rounds.

Not good. Eddie knew Sam, and he knew when his brother suspected something was amiss—which was almost never, considering Sam often struggled to identify and respond to human emotional responses in the first place. His brother was more machine than man sometimes, which meant that his focus on one particular matter that confused him could be all-encompassing, and he wouldn't let go until he had found a satisfactory explanation. If he thought something was off about Eddie, then he would investigate—and probably enlist Trinity along the way.

Eddie was eventually able to excuse himself to the bar for a drink, but the moment a cocktail waitress planted one down in front of him, he knew he wouldn't consume it. His stomach still churned with acid at the memory of last night's bender. He pushed the drink to the girl sitting beside him, ignored her expectant look, and signaled for a soda instead. The girl walked off with his drink as he took a long, appreciative sip of bar ginger ale. His stomach cooled, and he began turning over plans for how to duck out early.

His designs were interrupted as soon as he felt a pair of heavy eyes on him. Eddie turned on his stool.

Jonathan Daley—Margot's father—was staring at him from across the bar.

Of fucking *course* Jonathan would be in attendance. Hadn't Eddie sent him the invitation? Still, he'd been so preoccupied with Margot that the possibility of running into her father had completely escaped him until that moment.

For as long as Eddie had known him, Jonathan Daley had been a devoted family man—if a somewhat absent one. He was the owner of Daley Flights, a major airline company, so it made sense that he led a jet setting lifestyle that often left his wife and only daughter behind at home. He looked as if he could be a pilot himself: he was tall, good-looking and physically fit for his age, with a full head of short-cropped, distinguished white hair that made him stand out in any room. The hair was the first thing that Eddie recognized.

Jonathan inclined his head, and Eddie returned the subtle gesture with a nod of his own. Margot's father concluded the conversation he was having with a smile and crossed the room to meet him.

"Well, Eddie." Jonathan raised his beer in salutation and sat down without further invitation. Eddie shifted sideways needlessly to let him know he was welcome. "What do you intend to do about this situation?"

No segue. No real greeting or beating around the bush. No hour-long conversation spent digging for clues as to whether or not Mr. Daley wanted to bring it up. Eddie bit down on his tongue to keep it from wagging: *what situation?*

"Mr. Daley," he greeted. "I know you like a man who's always thinking ten steps ahead. And I just want you to know that I'm already planning for the future. *Our* future. I've already started doing research so Margot won't feel like she's alone in the planning process. In fact, I'm hoping to take most of it off her plate so she can focus on staying happy and healthy."

Eddie was privately pleased with the way he laid out his plans. He sounded self-assured; in-control; *mature.* He sounded completely unlike himself.

Though a part of him hated to think it, he sounded like his father.

If that really was the case, then maybe he risked presenting himself as too emotionally removed. Eddie leaned in a little, orbiting Jonathan's personal space without invading it. He pitched his voice lower. "Mr. Daley, I want you to know that I...I've always cared for Margot. More than I ever let on."

Jonathan leaned back a little—not to get away, Eddie thought, but to get a better look at him. He felt encouraged enough to continue. "I intend to ask her out officially the next time I see her. It's up to her, of course, whether or not she wants to date me, but I want to be involved in her life. *And* in the baby's life. Officially."

Jonathan barked a laugh, and some of the tension eased out of Eddie. He grinned as well, even if he didn't know what exactly they were laughing about. Maybe Mr. Daley was surprised by the fact that he had just stated his intentions, or maybe he was laughing with relief at Eddie's offer. Had they really expected him to *not* want to be involved in Margot's life?

"Oh, I think you can do better than *that,*" Jonathan said. He clapped a hand on Eddie's shoulder and took a sip of his beer.

Eddie blinked in confusion. "I can?"

Was it just him, or did the pressure of Jonathan Daley's fingers increase at his question?

"I certainly hope so," Jonathan said. "Because rest assured, that's not how I was envisioning things were going to happen between the two of you. I don't want you to *date* my daughter, Eddie. I think the time for courtship has long since passed."

"I…" Eddie didn't know what to say. So Jonathan *didn't* want him to try and start over with Margot? "I thought you would approve," he said.

"What I would approve of, Eddie, is you marrying my daughter." Jonathan's eyes lasered in on Eddie as Eddie choked. "And so would my wife."

"Marry Margot...?" The idea was terrifying. Not because Margot *wasn't* the type of woman he would want to marry. Actually, whenever Eddie had pictured himself settling down with a woman, he had always talked himself out of it by weighing that woman's traits against Margot's. Marrying Margot made sense, and he was surprised he hadn't thought about it more before now —but he was also privately alarmed that it had taken her father's interference to get him thinking along those lines. He felt like the situation was already spinning out of his control

"Leslie and I are what you call 'traditional'," Jonathan offered. He clapped Eddie on the shoulder again before pulling his hand back; he had kept a firm hold on him this entire time. "But not so traditional as to need the usual amount of time to plan things out. A few months should do the trick. After you propose, of course."

"Propose?" Eddie echoed hollowly.

"Why, sure!" Jonathan Daley's amiable laugh came again. "You know how to ask for a girl's hand, don't you? Maybe you can skip the sweeping gestures for the sake of expediency, hm? But an engagement ring wouldn't come amiss."

Eddie's throat silently worked as he processed all that Margot's father was saying. He knew negotiation; this was no negotiation. Jonathan fully expected him to follow the plan as outlined. "What if she says no?" he asked.

"Well then." Jonathan shrugged. "Margot has every right to refuse, of course. But then, I suppose you have every incentive to make sure she answers otherwise, don't you?" Jonathan's gaze was unflinching despite his casual tone, and Eddie felt caught in a steel trap. "I don't need to tell you that I have a multi-million dollar contract with your agency. I've stuck with you all this time to honor my commitment to your father...but the contract's coming up soon. I have no problem taking my business elsewhere, Eddie."

Eddie's throat was too dry to respond. He tried to summon up the lubrication to swallow; when none came, he settled for taking a long sip of his drink.

"Cheer up," Jonathan advised him. "Margot will say yes. After all, it would appear you certainly know how to be persuasive when it comes to matters involving my daughter, don't you, Eddie?"

"Yes, sir." He immediately wished he could take back his automatic assent. All he could do was wince at the way it hung in the air between them.

"So you'll be able to persuade her to marry right away," Jonathan continued. "And *before* anyone else finds out she's pregnant. You'll do everything in your power to provide for her every need. You'll make things right by her, Eddie. I know you will."

And you'll make things right by me, was Jonathan Daley's unspoken promise. *Or else.*

CHAPTER FOUR

EDDIE

E ddie sat, too stunned to move, agree, or protest the two possible futures Margot's father had just outlined for him.

He couldn't deny that it added up. Proposing marriage to Margot had never even crossed his mind, but now that Jonathan had laid it out for him...why hadn't he thought of it before? An official union would save Margot and her family from any potential embarrassment, and ensure that Eddie's own family—not to mention clients—understood that he really *had* turned over a new, more responsible leaf. Besides that, it would be the right thing to do. It would be a bigger gesture than the one he had planned originally, and a more total display of his commitment. Everyone would approve.

Jonathan was watching him process, before the buzzing of his cellphone drew his attention away. "I'll leave you to it," he said. "Just do my daughter a favor and don't think too long." Jonathan clapped him on the shoulder one last time in parting, and rose to go.

"Mr. Daley...just a second..."

Eddie moved to go after him, but a hand locked around his bicep and arrested him in place. He turned to find Sam staring at him with eyes as steely blue as his grip. There were two freshly-cracked beers already planted on the bar behind him.

"Sam. Shit."

"Sit down, Eddie," Sam advised.

"I'm hungover, remember?" Eddie gestured to the beer, but sat down anyway. He knew there was no escaping the conversation he was about to have. Judging by the look on Sam's face, his brother had already overheard everything.

"I don't care. Drink," Sam ordered.

Eddie complied. His stomach turned in momentary revolt as he took his first sip, but a cold, foamy beer wasn't a bad replacement for the soda he had been nursing all evening. He propped his elbows up on the bar alongside his brother and took a deep, measured breath.

Sam beat him to the punch. "Jonathan Daley is one tough bastard, huh?"

Eddie expelled his long breath in a surprised laugh. Of all the things he had expected Sam to say to him, he had *not* expected him to present himself as an ally. The evening was still early, and there was still plenty of time for Sam to shred him, but he felt more grateful than he knew how to express for his brother's opening remark.

"Yeah." Eddie raised his beer, and the two brothers clinked them together in solidarity. "I'm guessing you overheard everything," he added.

Sam nodded. "What are you going to do?"

"Isn't that the question?" Eddie laughed, but his mind was still spinning with everything that had happened to him in the past twenty-four hours. He wished he had Sam's uncanny ability to mentally parse and pursue the best course of action, but maybe sitting across from him at the bar was the second best thing. "What do you think I should do?

"You know I can't make that decision for you." Sam's piercing blue eyes studied him. "And I'm not going to bring company matters into this, either."

Eddie snorted, even though he could tell his brother was in earnest. Sam had only just recently learned to separate his personal life from his professional one, so to hear him promise as much now was certainly a gesture of love...even if it sounded unrealistic to Eddie. Did Sam really expect him *not* to factor Jonathan Daley's threat into his ultimate decision? He could weigh all the consequences and arrive at the best course of action to do right by everyone. He could multitask.

"Were you being truthful?" Sam prodded. "About caring for Margot all this time?"

"All this time." The confirmation should have come more readily, but Eddie still wasn't used to the torch he had always carried for Margot being semi-public knowledge. God, if he could have done this--*any* of this--differently, he would have planned it out better. He would have put his all into wooing the woman of his dreams and proving he wasn't the untamable, irre-sponsible man she thought he was. He would have made it easy, effortless, *right* for her to decide if she wanted to reciprocate. There wouldn't be an unexpected pregnancy, and all the outside duress that came with trying to do right by the baby while making everyone else happy. To his mind, Margot probably thought she had as few options as he did at this point. How could he be sure she would agree to marry him for the right reasons? What if she had already gotten him out of her system, or worse— what if her feelings for him had soured the moment those two pink strips materialized and changed the course of her life forever?

He would just have to cross that bridge when they came to it. He had already postponed meeting with her today, using the excuse of his hangover and the upcoming client mixer to hold off until next week. Maybe he was just a coward. Maybe he couldn't stand to know the truth of what Margot wanted.

All he could focus on now was what Margot *needed*.

"Do you want to marry her?" Sam's next question broke through his inner musings. Eddie blinked. He had almost forgotten where he was, and who he was with. That had been happening a lot since his passionate night with Margot two months ago. The woman his childhood friend had grown into was becoming all he could think about.

"I want a relationship with her," Eddie confirmed. "Her and the baby. I'm twenty-eight, Sam. Maybe it's time for me to grow up. Maybe that time is long overdue."

"Would you want all these same things even if there wasn't a baby in the equation?"

"I'm in...I've always loved Margot." Somehow it didn't sound as damning to phrase the truth differently. He wasn't lying, but he also wasn't highlighting a vulnerability. Margot needed someone she could depend on; not someone who had pined for years and wrapped himself up in less-storied drama with other women.

Sam nodded. He appeared satisfied with Eddie's responses so far, and Eddie couldn't help but wonder if it had all been a test. It would have been in line with the old Sam's character to conduct an interview on the subject and assess for himself if Eddie was qualified to take the next steps. "Can I offer you some advice?" Sam leaned back in his stool and crossed his arms, still holding his beer. Eddie took in the relaxed sight of his elder brother and felt his own posture loosen as a result. He couldn't believe he was sitting across from Sam receiving guidance rather than pissed-off directives.

"Please do."

"I haven't been in your situation," Sam said, "but that doesn't mean you can't learn from my mistakes. I nearly lost Trinity because I failed to listen to her...and I failed to follow her lead when it counted. We've been through a marriage, a divorce, and a reunion together, all because I didn't know when to let go. If you really have feelings for Margot, then you want a partnership with her."

"That's what I'm driving at," Eddie interrupted. "What better way to propose that partnership than marriage?"

Sam sighed. "But that's what I'm trying to tell you, Eddie. If you don't let her in on the conversation you just had with her father, you're already setting yourself up for failure. Margot *needs* to know what the stakes are, and she needs to know that it doesn't hold a candle to what the two of you share. You want to give her the choice to marry you, but is it a fully informed choice? You can't let your work obligations drive your relationship."

"I can juggle my obligations," Eddie promised. "You'll see.

I'm not going to let the agency fall by the wayside. And I'm sure as hell not going to let Margot go without a fight."

Sam's brow furrowed. "I'm not sure you're hearing me, Eddie."

"I'm hearing you, Sam," Eddie confirmed quickly. "Your work-life balance was out of whack. You forget that I had front row seats to all you and Trinity have gone through together. And you turned out all right in the end, didn't you?"

"Eddie…" Sam began warily, but Eddie could see it clearly now. Sam was afraid of watching his younger brother repeat his own relationship mistakes. This might be his only chance to allay Sam's fears before things with Margot started moving forward.

"Look, it's just like I told Jonathan. I've already started doing the research. I'm not going into this thing with Margot unprepared. Once she sees I'm in control of things, everything will fall into place exactly like we plan." Eddie took a long sip of his beer and expelled a heavy sigh. "The guy I used to be would have gone with the flow, but I promise you I intend to get out ahead of this situation. If there's one thing I've learned working on the fringes of the agency, it's that you can't forge forward and succeed without a plan. I'll arrange everything so it works out." He grinned. "I'm a Jameson, aren't I?"

"Sometimes I wonder what that means," Sam remarked. Eddie clapped his brother on the shoulder, imitating Jonathan Daley's easy body language in the face of the difficult conversation they had just concluded. He was feeling good, better than he had before. His hangover had almost dissipated, and hearing himself talk had assured him that he was ready to take this thing on. The old Eddie would have flown by the seat of his pants—or worse, sailed for Bali by now. He was a new man, a *better* man. He just had to stick to Jonathan's plan.

"Hey, Sam, thanks again for coming tonight. I appreciate it. I'm glad I have you on my side. You see? You didn't even have to offer me advice. I've got it all figured out. I'll just take after you, minus all the parts where you fucked up. If I approach the situation prepared, and stick with that plan, there's no way I can go wrong. Margot will see that."

Eddie took one last swig of his beer, sighed happily with his renewed conviction, and set it down on the bar.

Sam just shook his head. "Oh, how the tables have turned," he muttered, but Eddie couldn't imagine what he was talking about.

CHAPTER FIVE

MARGOT

M argot stared out at the heaving waves of the harbor. It was a crystal clear New York City day, and the water was bright and inviting with reflected sunlight. It wasn't nearly as dark and choppy as usual; in fact, by harbor standards it was borderline tranquil.

Her stomach still revolted at the sight. Maybe agreeing to a tete-a-tete on Eddie's boat hadn't been such a hot idea after all.

She hadn't been surprised when Eddie rescheduled their "meeting". There wasn't a doubt in her mind that he hadn't returned to the Thirty Under Thirty party after taking her home and drank himself well past the legal limit at the news of her pregnancy. At least she trusted him to be responsible enough to call for a cab in the post-chivalrous hours of his night. She had seen firsthand the drunken mischief an intoxicated Eddie could get up to...and what the earth-shattering consequences could be.

Not that *she* was off the hook by any stretch. Hell, when you got right down to it she put the "hook" in "ill-advised hookup".

Margot cradled her stomach thoughtfully. It was a habit she had already formed, even though she wasn't showing any physical signs of pregnancy yet. Nothing aside from the nausea, anyway.

She keyed in the code Eddie had texted her earlier and let herself into the private dock. No one came to meet her as she walked down the ramp alone. Maybe Eddie was a no-show. A part of her hoped that he was. She was terrified of setting foot on his expensive ship and losing her lunch.

She tried not to imagine she was walking the plank as she approached the boat on the end. Eddie's ship was small and sleek; it was named *Annabella*, after his long-deceased mother. Margot's own memories of Annabella were fuzzy, but she remembered that Eddie's mother had always been a warm and caring presence, one that slipped fresh cookies to a visiting Margot and still commanded the respect of her houseful of rambunctious boys.

Just the sight of the boat rocking on the water now made Margot freeze mid-step. She hastily fished through her purse for the sleeve of saltines she had started to carry with her. Recently her bouts of morning sickness were hitting her during the day, and she was hoping to avoid causing a scene. She found that crackers always helped settle her stomach.

"Unforgettable...that's what you are...unforgettable..."

Nat King Cole's rich voice wafted to her. Margot glanced up, startled, and several crackers spilled from her hand. A seagull alighted on a nearby post and squawked eagerly, but came no closer as she strained her ears to listen.

"Like a song of love that clings to me...how the thought of you does things to me..."

She was five years old again. Annabella's radio was on in the kitchen, and Eddie was walking her down the "aisle"—the name that young Margot had given to the long hallway leading to the Jamesons' back porch. Eddie held her hand aloft in his, and gamely spun her around every time they reached the end of the hall to begin their wedding march anew. She had Annabella's apron tied around her head and flowing down her back like a bridal veil.

When Nat King Cole's velvet crooning inevitably faded to commercial, they would pause and turn to one another, joining their hands with sober expressions. Sometimes Eddie would keep a stolen twist tie in his pocket to wrap around her ring finger. "Margie," he would ask her, "will you marry me?"

"I do," she would confirm dutifully. It was just another game, a script memorized between them. Whenever they got to the only part of their wedding vows they knew well enough to recite —*"you may now kiss the bride"*—they would lean in with their lips puckered, then thrust one another away before they could *actually* kiss, laughing uproariously at the narrowly avoided gross-out.

Margot blinked herself back to the present. She glanced up, and saw a broad-shouldered silhouette watching her from the prow of the ship. She shaded her eyes, and her thudding heart picked up the pace as every handsome detail of Eddie Jameson materialized. He looked older, and oddly regal, standing so high above her. Either he was absurdly overdressed, or her sweatshirt and jeans weren't the casual boating attire she had thought they were. Eddie was wearing a crisp black suit and long pants; no open shirt, no shorts. His auburn hair was slicked back, and even standing dockside, Margot could tell he was sporting the closest shave he had ever worn since picking up a razor in high school. It was the most she had ever seen him look to his older brother, Sam. The resemblance was almost jarring.

Maybe he really did plan to treat this like a business meeting.

"You're late!" he called out down to her. He leaned forward to brace himself on the bulwark.

Margot checked her phone. She was exactly on time. She wondered if Eddie had been driving himself crazy below deck all morning stewing on the exact words he would say to her, and wasn't sure how to take the mental image. Eddie wasn't usually a planner. "You rescheduled on me first!" she called back. She tossed the rest of her crackers toward the waiting seagull and moved around the side of the boat.

Eddie came to meet her. Margot mounted the stepstool, and he extended his hand down to her to help her up. She wished her heart didn't somersault at the gesture. She could still hear the radio playing in the galley, and it suddenly occurred to her that Eddie might have made his music selection on purpose.

"You look well-rested," he mentioned as he hauled her up. Margot clutched her purse close to keep it from falling into the water below her. *Don't look down, don't look down,* she prayed. "Better than the last time I saw you."

"And you look like your brother," she pointed out. She glanced around *Annabella's* deck in an effort to avoid noticing the rocking waves beneath them, and her mouth dropped open. "Eddie…? What is this?"

The entire deck was carpeted with dark red rose petals, the exact color of Margot's favorite sultry lipstick. A bottle of sparkling cider perched sweating in a bucket of ice on the outdoor table; twin crystalline wine glasses flashed in the light of the sun.

There was a teal blue Tiffany box sitting on the chair canted closest to her.

"That's why, darling, it's incredible...that someone so unforgettable...thinks that I am unforgettable too."

Margot's hand flew to her mouth. Eddie came up behind her, but she couldn't bring herself to tear her gaze away from the scene. Everything clicked into place suddenly. She was an idiot not to see it before.

"Well?" His voice was a seductive purr right next to her ear. "What do you think? Or are you speechless? I can work with silence. I'll even take it as encouraging if you don't mind."

Something was building inside of Margot...something *not* good. She felt faint, fluttery. Her lower back and armpits tingled; a buzzing sensation erupted between her eyes.

"Why don't you go look at your gift?" Eddie encouraged. "Better yet, why don't I bring it to you?" He touched her shoulder affectionately as he moved past her to go retrieve the blue box. Another, much larger ship was pulling out of the harbor. It honked a low, mournful signal that drowned out the climax of Nat King Cole's "Unforgettable".

The boat left a massive wake trailing behind it.

The deck pitched beneath her, and Margot groped behind her for the hand railing. Eddie made it to the table without so much as a hitch in his confident stride. His sea legs really were out of this world. He moved so gracefully on the water, so naturally. He was the same way in social situations—nobody could breeze through a crowd like Eddie and come away with exactly what he wanted.

He pulled the lid off the box and set it aside. Margot watched, with eyes she was sure were as round as the dinner platters he had set out for them, as Eddie removed a velvet ring box. He returned and knelt before her. He took her hand in his. His palm was so tan and wide it practically dwarfed her own. She looked so pale by comparison. Had her skin always been this clammy? Eddie didn't appear to notice anything amiss. "Margot Daley, ever since we were kids, I've found you unforgettable," he began. "I spent so much of my childhood running around playing games with you. When you weren't there, all I could think about was the next time I would see you again. I was devoted to you. I still am."

Stop. Stop it, Eddie. She was desperate to absorb everything he was saying to her, but she couldn't concentrate. This wasn't the old script, and Eddie…Eddie didn't sound like himself. What's more, his timing couldn't have been any worse. Her stomach rolled as if there were smaller waves pitching inside of it. Her hand stayed resolutely clamped over her mouth.

It was like watching a slow motion train wreck.

"Margot Daley, if it isn't obvious by now, I want to ask for your hand in marriage," Eddie was saying. If she had the courage to take her hand away in that moment, she would have knocked some sense into him. All of this over an unplanned pregnancy? Was Eddie out of his mind? He gazed up at her, his brown eyes serious and expectant.

It was too much.

"I'm sorry, Eddie." Margot only barely managed to get the apology out as she pulled her hand from his.

She turned, and retched over the side of the boat.

She continued to heave for several moments after she had finished. Tears stung the corners of her eyes. *Rotten morning sickness.* Eddie had gone through so much trouble to surprise her by setting up this "meeting", and she couldn't handle standing upright through one measly boat wake…

When Margot finally regained enough composure to turn back around, she found that Eddie had disappeared below deck. She pushed several strands of hair out of her eyes and exhaled in disappointment. She didn't know whether to feel more frustrated or relieved that his stilted attempts to propose had been inter-rupted. All of this...cliché...it was so *not* the Eddie Jameson she knew. And it definitely wasn't the Eddie Jameson who made her heart race with his unexpected antics. That boy was the one she had once dreamed of marrying: the one who promoted his total zest for life, and dragged others along with him into adventure.

When Eddie reappeared moments later, he wasn't carrying a bouquet of exotic flowers or a glossy-furred Golden Retriever puppy with a bow around its neck. He was carrying a grocery bag. Before Margot could puzzle out the situation, or trust herself enough to open her mouth and ask, Eddie was ushering her back off the boat to the relative stability of the dock.

The last thing she expected once they arrived was to find a carton of yogurt thrust into her hands. She blinked her astonish-ment in what must have been Morse code. "Oh, right." Eddie fished around his pockets and produced a small silver spoon. He passed it to her. "Here. Eat. Protein helps," he explained.

Margot gazed at him in wonderment. "You...did you really stock the fridge of your ship with *yogurt?* Just for me?"

"I have other stuff, too," Eddie said quickly. "Everything from ginger root to ginger ale if you're feeling nauseous. I can even make you a peanut butter and banana sandwich. I know you used to like those when we were growing up."

Margot's face heated. "I'm not a kid anymore, Eddie." Somehow it felt important to convey as much. She wanted him to think of her as her own woman, and not some sepia-colored photograph of a childhood obligation.

He watched her as she spooned a dollop of yogurt past her lips. It felt like the bravest thing she had done all morning. Her stomach gave a sharp twist as she swallowed, but almost immediately after she felt her insides overcome by a cool, soothing sensation. She closed her eyes and breathed in deeply through her nose. When she opened them again, she noticed Eddie staring at her.

"I know you're not a kid, Margot." His hand touched her waist, almost shy in its hesitance. She knew she should pull away —at the very least to spare him if her stomach decided it still had more left in it to evacuate—but she did the exact opposite. She leaned in.

"What do you want from me, Eddie Jameson?"

"I want you to marry me," he replied. "I'm not above asking you again."

Margot could scarcely believe what he was saying. "Two marriage proposals in the same day?" she asked. She was trying to play it off lightly, but there was no easy joke to be found in their exchange.

"In the same day," Eddie confirmed. He smiled crookedly. "I never got a proper answer from you before."

"Maybe that's because I've never experienced a proper offer before." She knew she was stalling, and a part of her suspected that Eddie must know the same. This was all so sudden. First the unexpectedness of their one-night stand; then the baby; now marriage? It felt like the world's cruelest nursery rhyme played in reverse. *First comes the baby carriage, then comes marriage, then comes...?*

Did Eddie love her? Margot paused, her spoon hovering over the yogurt. When she next summoned the courage to glance up, she found Eddie watching her intently. "Eddie, I…"

He must have seen something in her face that encouraged him, although Margot couldn't imagine what. Her head was as turned around as her stomach, and even she didn't know how she intended to complete her sentence.

But when Eddie sensed an opening, he took it. He withdrew the clamshell Tiffany box from his pocket a second time and popped it open. Margot stared in disbelief at the diminutive ring that glinted at her, nestled in its velvet cushion. It was the most perfect princess cut diamond she had ever laid eyes on. It seemed to wink at her, its square edges understated yet somehow regal in their dimensions. The architect in her couldn't help but appreciate Eddie's aesthetic choice, even if the woman in her had never imagined herself becoming a bride. Not recently, anyway.

She still couldn't shake the memory of playing 'wedding' with a young Eddie Jameson. Wasn't this the natural conclusion to her childhood fantasy? Deep down, wasn't this what she had always wanted all along?

"I've always cared for you, Margot." He seemed to articulate her thoughts aloud now, and Margot froze. Eddie stepped nearer to her. "Maybe this baby is a sign. Maybe we really should consider joining our lives together. What do you say?"

Margot looked from the ring, to the yogurt, and back again. When her eyes finally alighted on one thing and one thing only, she beheld the image of Eddie Jameson: the boy she had known since childhood, all grown up now and ready to take the next terrifying leap into adulthood. Neither of them was prepared for this; she could see it in his face, despite his best attempts to hide his own misgivings. She knew him too well to not recognize the signs. His bold eyebrows knit together over the proud jut of his nose, and his lips held a smile that simply didn't match up with the concern his melting brown eyes were expressing. Two of the three Jameson boys were capable of poker faces in her experience, and Eddie wasn't one of them.

"Eddie…" Margot trailed off. She was suddenly unsure if she had the words to properly convey how much he meant to her, and how terrified she was of committing without the time to think first. He seemed to have it all figured out—*Eddie Jameson* seemed to have a plan for this. Did she? A year or two ago, the old Margot would have obsessed over every little detail until it was perfect.

But nothing about this situation with Eddie was perfect.

*And yet...*a part of her whispered. *And yet...*

And yet this was *the* boy, the one she had always loved, and never found a way to express as much. Somehow, the yogurt meant more to her than the peerless, priceless ring that glimmered just out of reach of her finger.

"All right," she said. "Why not? Let's give this marriage thing a shot."

It was probably the most anticlimactic form her answer could have taken, but Eddie expelled a long sigh of relief, and Margot realized she might have just single-handedly taken the weight of the world off his shoulders.

She tried not to notice how heavy the ring felt as he slipped it on her finger.

CHAPTER SIX

EDDIE

The last thing Eddie expected to do when he showed up at the bridal salon that afternoon was to cause a sensation.

He had too much on his mind to *really* take notice of the female attention he was receiving, much less let it go to his head. He was a father and a fiancé now; the old Eddie need not apply.

Still, it had taken him an embarrassing amount of time to recognize what everybody else was looking at. He arrived before Margot, and promptly introduced himself to the consultant he had spoken with over the phone. Zelma was a slender woman, maybe forty, with intelligent blue eyes framed by glasses; she didn't seem one to suffer nonsense, a type that usually steered clear of Eddie, but she had let her hand linger in Eddie's for longer than was expressly necessary to complete a handshake. All the other female employees of the salon, too, had taken turns indiscreetly peeking out from the front desk and around the door of the breakroom as Eddie followed Zelma through a head-spinning wonderland of glistening white fabric.

His head had yet to stop spinning since that fateful night with Margot.

"We will stick to the muumuus, then," Zelma was saying. "If what you say is true, and your bride will be showing by the time you walk her down the aisle.

Eddie nodded gratefully. He was glad he had thought to mention it. That was one less thing Margot would have to worry about; he had already narrowed their choices and expedited the process.

"And over here, you'll find we have a gorgeous selection of sheer nighties for the bride-to-be...forgive me for presuming, but I thought I would give you a brief tour before she arrives, in case you wanted to surprise her on your wedding night."

"Good thinking," Eddie said. His eyes lingered on the tantalizing array before him, and he reached out to finger the nearest number and see for himself just how translucent the fabric was when paired with human skin. He hadn't even *thought* about the wedding night.

"If your fiancé doesn't show…" One of the salon girls surprised him by appearing to volunteer her services. Eddie turned to her and arched an eyebrow; two other female employees half-hidden behind an open fitting room door giggled and receded as if they were working. He wondered if he had inadvertently become the subject of a dare.

Evidently his consultant wondered also. "You. Take these to the other room." Zelma unloaded what must have been five different wedding dresses into the girl's arms. "And *shoo.*" She spoke with a tart accent he didn't recognize, but he thought she might be German. Then again, maybe it was only the tone of reprimand that made him think so.

The fitting room was unrecognizable by the time he returned to it. There were dresses piled everywhere, hanging off of doors and partitions, and it appeared that extra mannequins had been hauled in from the back and draped in wedding finery. It looked like a snowstorm had blown through and deposited an avalanche. Eddie rubbed the back of his neck and contemplated voicing concern; Zelma noticed, and simply shook her head.

"I assure you, Mr. Jameson, it is a normal amount. Can I get you a Perrier?"

"Sure," Eddie said. He thought Zelma was probably also looking for an excuse to chastise her employees, but waved her off to let her know he would survive a minute without her. He felt momentarily relieved to be left alone...before realizing that he wasn't *supposed* to be doing this alone. He couldn't do any of the actual trying-on—although that would certainly expedite the process at this point.

"Come on, Margot." Eddie checked his watch again. Margot was late, and he was getting antsy. He hadn't planned for the possibility that she might be a no-show, but now the dread was creeping up on him. Margot was usually so on top of things, but lately she seemed off her game. Eddie liked to think he understood completely—and that the new role he inhabited in her life enabled him to pick up the slack—but what if Margot's distraction came from a place he hadn't anticipated? What if she was already getting cold feet?

If Margot backed out of the engagement, then *he* would be the one responsible for losing the Daley account. Eddie had done some snooping—which mainly involved calling up Trinity and asking for info he hadn't kept up with during his prodigal years abroad—and had confirmed his suspicion that Daley Flights was currently the agency's biggest client. They had maintained the number one spot for almost all his years of existence. Sam of all people had tried to downplay it the other night, as if Eddie could genuinely afford to lose them Jonathan Daley's business.

Panic was setting in. He could feel it crawling up his throat; he was afraid that if he opened his mouth, he'd accidentally shout in primal dismay, or worse, call the whole thing off. Eddie swallowed the sensation back down quickly, and smoothed a thumb across one eyebrow. He was perfectly in control.

"Eddie?"

It was *her* voice. His bride-to-be. Suddenly, Eddie didn't need to establish appearances or coping mechanisms; a feeling of instant relief washed over him, and he turned with his arms already spread to greet Margot.

"Your kingdom, my queen."

Margot snorted. She was wearing a short red sleeveless dress, and there was a black belt cinched around her waist. Her beautiful long legs extended downward to a pair of matching heels. She balanced a small purse on her shoulder, and the hand clenched over the strap wore his ring. His heart jolted at the sight. He still wasn't used to seeing it there, nestled between her pinky and middle finger.

"Hey, relax. I already did most of the hard part for you." Eddie stepped to her and pulled her hand free, sealing it between both of his. "White-knuckle that purse any more and you'll turn that diamond ring into a lump of coal."

Margot compressed her lips and gave a little laugh through her nose. "I knew you flunked geology, Eddie. I just didn't realize you flunked it *that* badly."

He watched her take in the array of dresses. He waited, half-expectant, for the inkling of a smile.

When it never came, he realized suddenly that this may have been a bad idea.

"Sorry. I didn't mean to inundate you with e-mails all week," he said as he led her deeper into the dressing room. "I knew blasting your inbox with wedding plans was probably a risky maneuver, but..."

I wanted you to feel like I was taking charge. Not exactly something he could openly admit to a girl like Margot. She was fiercely independent, what he had once heard his father call a 'ball-buster', and that had been when they were *six*. He had to mold himself into the right man for her without too obviously letting onto the fact.

Easier said than done.

"No. I...really appreciate your maneuver, Eddie. *All* of your maneuvers." Margot waved to the dresses scattered around the room. Zelma chose that moment to return, and momentarily spared Eddie from trying to unpack the meaning behind Margot's words.

"Beautiful bride," Zelma said approvingly. She passed them both a bottle of mineral water and gestured toward the dresses. "Shall we get started?"

"Might as well make a dent," Eddie agreed as he sat down. He was suddenly too nervous to twist the top off his water, much less take a drink. "Margot?"

"I'm on it." She grinned and gave him a game thumbs-up. The feeling of ease that just having her around returned to him, and Eddie laughed. Zelma didn't appear to appreciate them making light of her mountainous piles of dresses, but the consultant only thinned her lips and nodded. She selected one off the top and accompanied Margot behind the fitting room screen.

An hour later, and their spirits were starting to dwindle. Eddie kept an encouraging smile plastered to his face as Margot reappeared in—was this dress five? *Ten?*—a monstrous white ensemble, looking for all the world like a deflated balloon. As the consultant bent to study something around the hem of the sequined skirt, Margot's wild eyes sought and found his. She mouthed something that looked like a plea for help; she clamped her teeth shut once more as Zelma rose. Her smile for the consultant looked excruciatingly painful.

"These muumuu-style dresses are very beautiful," Zelma said as Margot made a first, second, and third pass before the mirrors. "So girlish. So modest."

So not Margot, Eddie felt like volunteering. He watched her turn repeatedly; to the outside observer, it looked like she was desperately hunting for an angle she found flattering. He would never admit it out loud with their consultant in the room, but the dresses so far all looked awful hanging off Margot's slender frame. She might as well be trying on an assortment of high-end trash bags.

"It's…" Margot fished for a word and came up short.

Eddie turned to their consultant. "Zelma? Can we have a minute?"

Zelma nodded. "Of course. I will be just outside the door if you need anything."

As soon as she had vanished from view, Eddie rose and crossed to Margot. Now that the consultant was out of the room, Margot's proud posture deteriorated to a slump. Eddie put his arm around her bowed shoulders, and turned her face away from the mirrors with a gentle finger guiding her chin.

"Margot," he whispered, "you can talk to me. Tell me what's wrong." He hated seeing her like this. Was it the baby? The wedding? Was it *him?* He dreaded hearing any or all of the above, but he'd rather she plunge the whole handful of emotional knives through his heart than hold back at this point. He would rather take on the pain than see her crestfallen look now.

"It's just that...I had sort of envisioned wearing something different on the big day," she admitted. "These dresses are wonderful, Eddie. Really. But you know better than anyone how I used to drag you into playing out all my wedding fantasies when we were kids. I thought I grew out of them, but..." She shook her head. "God, I remember how much space it used to occupy in my little brain. I had oodles of drawings describing how I thought my dress would look. And these..."

"Are hideous," Eddie supplied.

Margot nodded gratefully and chuckled.

"I should have known better," he said. "I wouldn't have let any of these—what did she call them, muumuus?—near you. Wait right here." He pulled his arm from her shoulders and went to relay this latest information to Zelma in the hallway. After a thoughtful moment, the consultant nodded and disappeared back inside the store. Moments later, she returned with an armful of

48

dress that, to Eddie, looked identical to all the others. When he opened his mouth to protest, Zelma shook her head.

"Wait," she advised him. She passed the dress off to Margot; the latter shot Eddie a desperate look. Surely Zelma's selection had come too easily to be correct. Eddie just shrugged and sat down. As much as he tried to help, he knew he was ultimately useless when it came to this sort of thing. He was willing to try just about anything at this point if it meant putting a smile back on Margot's face.

Moments later, when Margot stepped from behind the partition, he lurched back out of his seat.

"Margot!" Eddie blinked, and his eyes raked her figure. After all the previous failures, he hadn't expected to be dazzled by the vision of her in the dress, but *this...*this was something else.

Margot laced her hands together in front of herself and grinned. The gown she wore was so pristinely white its shadows held an almost blue edge. The slightest tilt of her body caused the sequins of the embroidered bodice to catch the light and cast resplendent, dancing motes upon the wall. The heart-shaped top of the bodice perfectly cradled her breasts, while also pushing them proudly forward; the deep valley of her cleavage made his pulse triple, and he quickly raised his eyes to take in the rest of her. Without sleeves, Margot's sun-kissed shoulders and elegant bare arms were on full display. This gown may have been tighter than all the others, but it allowed her to move and breathe in a way he hadn't seen all afternoon. Margot looked at home; the dress looked as if it had been made for her.

"Well?" Her thickly-lashed hazel eyes looked bigger than

usual; they looked hopeful. Expectant. Somewhere behind him, Zelma gave a low whistle.

"Margot, I..." He had no words. He was struck dumb by the sight of her. All he could do was reach forward, and offer her his hand to help her up onto the platform at the center of all the mirrors. Margot rose to the occasion and stared at herself. She looked as if she didn't recognize her own face in the mirror. *No, Eddie thought. That isn't right. It's the girl who always played wedding finally meeting the bride.*

"...I wanted to say you look like an angel," he continued after a long moment. "But that isn't a satisfactory comparison. You look like Heaven, Margot."

Her eyes glistened, and she glanced down quickly to smooth her hands along the bodice. When she had composed herself, she sighed. "It really was a nice fantasy, Eddie...but you know I won't fit in this by the time our wedding day arrives." She turned to him and smiled sadly. "Thanks for making all my childhood daydreams a reality, even for a moment."

Her certainty was almost enough to break his heart on the spot. Eddie wanted to leap up; he wanted to explain her father's ultimatum; he wanted to take his beautiful bride-to-be in his arms and kiss her senseless. He wanted to tell her they could still seize the fantasy and make the big day completely their own despite all the outside pressures that had started the ball rolling in the first place.

But he knew that he couldn't bring the truth into it now. The moment Margot realized this wedding wasn't his idea was the moment she confirmed for herself that he wasn't in control. He *wanted* her to think he had arrived at the idea to propose on his own. There wasn't a doubt in his mind that it was the right thing to do, and that it was the thing he *wanted* to do. So did it really make a difference whose idea it was?

Maybe it does, and maybe it doesn't, a nagging voice whispered in the back of his brain. *But maybe what matters most is that your white wedding is about to be founded on a little white lie of omission.*

"Margot." Eddie stepped to the pedestal she stood atop, allowing his hands to alight on her curves. The dress she wore felt as good as it looked; the bodice hugged her trim waist and practically trumpeted the existence of her womanly dips and swells. He skimmed his fingers up towards her ribcage. Margot hummed with appreciation, sounding a little like a cat on the receiving end of a familiar caress. The noise made Eddie want to banish Zelma from the room, and undo all of Margot's hard work trying on dresses by completely stripping her of clothing. Whatever she thought of the body that lay beneath her dress, he could conceive of a dozen ways to show her his appreciation for it.

"Yes, Eddie?" Her breath caught a little as he smoothed his fingers down the fabric of her skirt.

"We don't have to wait to get married," he stated. "We can get married two months from now. Hell, we can get married next month."

"Are you serious?" Her eyebrows shot up. "You don't think that's too soon?"

Your father certainly doesn't. "Why not?" he asked instead. "You can wear the dress of your dreams. You can have the *wedding* of your dreams."

"It's too fast," Margot replied dubiously. "Even two months is…"

"Just leave all the planning to me," he jumped in quickly. "I want your input, of course, to make sure I'm on the right track. But the timing...and all the technical stuff...I want you to let *me* be the one to worry about it."

Margot's hand caught his and closed over it. She was white-knuckling again. Eddie sensed that she was waging an internal battle, but over what? Was she having trouble letting go of all the responsibility that usually fell to her—and could he really blame her for feeling nervous letting him take the lead on this one? He didn't have the best reputation when it came to planning, much less execution.

Or did Margot's hesitance stem from something else?

"Go with the flow," he heard her breathe to herself. She relaxed her grip on his hand, but Eddie squeezed her fingers before she could release him. "All right, Eddie. If you think it's doable...and if you think it's a good idea…"

"I think it's a good idea you wear *that* dress," Eddie said. "You look hot as hell, Margie. You might burn the church down by accident."

It was the right thing to say. "You think so?" she laughed. She practically melted into his hands, and Eddie couldn't restrain himself any longer. He pulled her down off the pedestal and in against his chest; after a moment, he let her slide slowly to the floor. He was enjoying the feel of her in his arms a little too much, and found that now that he had her, he had no immediate plans to let her go. Zelma cleared her throat and turned her back to allow them a bit of privacy.

"Thanks, Eddie." Margot's beautiful face beamed up at him, and for a moment he forgot how to breathe. When she raised herself up on her toes, he knew he was in danger of never relearning. She touched his face tenderly, then canted her head and leaned in.

Margot's kiss was completely unexpected. Her lips grazed his, and he gave a startled, sharp intake of breath; before he could voice his surprise, or do something equally idiotic to ruin the moment, she pressed in closer and wrapped her arms around his neck. He could feel the line of her smile, and the way her lips still pouted generously enough to meet with his. His hands found her waist, and he yanked her in roughly against him. Minutes ago, a part of him had been afraid of letting his need show; now, he wanted Margot to feel *exactly* what seeing her in that dress had done to him. His cock stirred to life beneath his belt, and her tongue flicked past her lips to give his own tongue a playful taste.

She pulled back before he could lose his senses completely. Now it was Eddie's turn to clear his throat and turn away as Margot addressed Zelma.

"I really feel as if I could inspire a standing ovation in this dress." She dropped a wink as Eddie coughed. "I think we'll take it."

CHAPTER SEVEN

MARGOT

Margot had been the inspiration for one of Eddie's *standing ovations* before. She sat alone in the backseat on the car ride home from the salon, gazing out the window at the bright smear of city lights. She had borrowed one of her father's cars for the time being; generally, Margot liked to exert her independence (and daring, her mother seemed to think) by taking cabs and Ubers, but ever since word of her pregnancy had gotten out to her parents, they had insisted on chauffeuring her around. Margot found that she didn't mind it as much as she did when she was a teenager: the driver was always professional, and always silent. Her rides around the city allowed her some much-needed time to think.

To reflect.

It was getting harder and harder to resist the pull of reliving her first night with Eddie. As much as she tried to exist solely for the 'here' and the 'now' and not worry about the future, that philosophy was a recent development. The old Margot—the

Margot of only a few months ago—would have been five steps ahead of Eddie already, making sure every appointment was in place, making sure *he* was on-time and mentally present.

Boy, how things have changed.

Margot sank back into the cushiony upholstery and let the flashing city lights lull her. They reminded her of the colorful flashing of the expensive drinks ferried by the waiters at the party… the party…

Her father's party had been in full swing by the time Eddie Jameson arrived: late, as usual. It gave him an excuse to wear that puppy dog look that begged forgiveness--his second best look. Margot had known Eddie arrived before she even laid eyes on him. There was always a change in the air, a noticeable shift, whenever a Jameson brother showed to a party, and Eddie's aura was distinctive. Even the soberest member of the New York City old money elite couldn't help lighting up a little, or letting slip a chuckle that sounded dusty from disuse, at something Eddie said or did.

When she finally caught sight of him, he was already looking at her…or drinking her in, Margot felt, with a blush at the memory. His eyes had burned so hot, and his thoughts had been broadcast so plainly on his face, that for a moment she had looked away to make sure her father wasn't in the vicinity to see. Then she had navigated toward him through the room full of crowded bodies.

By the time she arrived, Eddie was wearing his first best look: he smoldered. And Margot felt herself begin to heat on the inside by proximity to him. They didn't stray far from one another's side for the rest of the evening. Even when he was engaging in conversation with a different group than her, Eddie kept his finger hooked in her sleeve. The wine flowed. She started ordering her drinks on the rocks.

Then, when there was a lull in the attention being paid them, Margot and Eddie had slipped out.

She still remembered the way they had stumbled, giggling, against the threshold to her room. Eddie had put out a hand to prevent her from striking her temple against the doorframe, and Margot... Margot had surged upward the moment he brought himself within kissing distance. Their mouths had collided imperfectly, needfully...but it didn't matter. It was their first kiss, yet they had mapped each other's lips so many times before with their eyes, it felt like a joyful homecoming.

Eddie had backed her into her bedroom. He had never been inside it before, but he seemed to know the layout just fine in the dark. His intuition carried them to the bed. His hands stripped the straps of Margot's dress from her shoulders, and reached around back to unhook the secret bra in almost the same sweep. His lips never relented. He kissed her neck as if he wanted to devour every inch of her. "You smell so good," she recalled him murmuring, and it sent a shiver racing down her spine to hear the echo of his words even now. Alcohol may have muddled their decisions that night, but every meaningful moment came into crystal-clear focus still. She recalled the way he had let her bra slip from her breasts, and how its descent had mirrored her own slow fall back down onto the bed. She had found herself caged by the arms she had caught herself admiring more and more the older they got; when she reached out a hand to squeeze a band of muscle, he flexed in response.

She remembered that Eddie had fallen back on his haunches. His hands had slid up the lean plane of her stomach to palm her breasts; he held them for a moment, as if he couldn't believe he was really touching them, before gripping with surprising possession. *Mine*, his hands seemed to suggest, and Margot had arched into him in response.

Yours, her body agreed. *All along I've been yours.*

When he could bring himself to let go of her breasts—they were peaked and aching from the teasing of his fingers—Eddie rocked back again and whipped off his dinner jacket. What followed was a jumble of limbs and laughter as they speedily untangled themselves from their remaining clothing. Evidence of the formal evening lay on the floor beside the bed.

The bed rocked beneath them. Eddie pinned her wrists, kissing every inch of her as if she was a hors d'oeuvre he had brought home from the party to relish in private. Margot writhed and struggled and *laughed* beneath him, until a steely look crossed his face, one she had never seen before. Her laughter dissolved to disbelieving moans after that as his mouth laid claim to her by inches. By the time he had arrived at the bed of curls nestled between her legs, she was shuddering with the intensity of her need.

His tongue flicked along the inner folds of her labia as he continued his private tasting. Margot sighed happily and lay back, letting her head fall against the pillow. He swirled his tongue, then thrust, pushing hard against her clit, making her breath catch and her voice soar with the height of her need. When she couldn't take anymore, she reached down for him and pulled him back up to kiss him fervently. She remembered their bodies shifting, Eddie bracing himself...

And then he had entered her. The first moments of sex had never felt so goddamn *good*, and Margot wondered if they ever would again with a man who wasn't Eddie Jameson. The tension, the torment, she had felt every time she looked at him, melted away in one hot rush. His cock was thick and seemed to almost pulse within her—or was that her own heartbeat?

When he began thrusting between her legs, she thought she would hit the roof. She grabbed for his shoulders; they were already slick with perspiration, but at least it was something to hold onto. The bed lurched beneath them and knocked against the wall. She cried and begged and pleaded incoherently, but Eddie seemed to know exactly what it was she sought. At every turn he found a new angle, a new rhythm, that no lover before him had been intuitive enough to discover... and Margot knew she was done. No man would ever outmatch him in her bedroom. This might be her only hit and she was already addicted.

When she came, her knees quaked, and she clenched her thighs around his surging hips. Eddie kept pumping, prolonging her release, making her cry his name again and again until he groaned her own in answer. He had come in a hot jet—she had felt his seed rush deep inside her—but she hadn't thought of anything at the time except how good it felt and how complete she was.

They had fallen, spent and laughing, into a sweaty heap. The ceiling above Margot spun, but she hadn't been certain it was the alcohol making the world whirl. She had half-expected Eddie to try and stumble back into his clothes and out the door, so that any suspicion of their night together might be avoided; instead, he had thrown an arm over her, pinning her to the bed, and lost himself in kissing her shoulder until he fell asleep. She had tried to remain awake beneath him, to memorize every breath, every detail, but had found herself slipping hopelessly into unconsciousness before long…

"… miss?"

Margot blinked slowly. The car had stopped moving. The driver was standing at her elbow now, the door pulled open, revealing a snapshot of familiar curb. Her apartment building loomed large above the street. It was a beautiful, efficient building. Margot wouldn't have lived in any other kind.

But looking at it now, she couldn't help thinking how lonely it was. Efficiency had a price, and it was one she was tired of paying. She wanted to throw the schedule out and embrace life— she wanted to be more like Eddie. It was something she had decided the morning after they had spent the night together, the morning after the best sex of her life.

There had to be a reason Eddie was so happy and free, and she wanted to know the secret. Just loving him, secretly and to herself, wasn't enough. To be the best match for him, in that wide world of women he had such intimate knowledge of, she would have to emulate him. She *would* go with the flow.

And she had no doubt that flow would take her to Eddie in the end.

CHAPTER EIGHT

EDDIE

"...**E**ddie, *relax,*" Margot whispered from the examination chair. "They're just doing an ultrasound."

Eddie was on edge, and everyone in the room knew it. The doctor spent half her time soothing him when her attention should have been solely focused on Margot, but he couldn't seem to stop drawing the focus away. He tried to relax, and wound up nearly coming off of his stool in the process.

"Here you go, sweetie." Another nurse entered and brought him a cup of water. Eddie accepted, but tried to offer it to Margot first; she just shook her head, looking bemused. He downed it in one gulp and crumpled the cup in his fist.

"You took that water like you take your shots," Margot noticed.

"I just...I guess I wasn't expecting this," Eddie said. How was he supposed to tell Margot, laid out and vulnerable, that this ultrasound was something out of the ordinary? Why didn't the doctor say as much? Wasn't that her job?

Margot raised an eyebrow. "I thought you said you read up on all this stuff?"

He didn't want to alarm her, but he now felt as if he had no choice. "I did. All my research indicated that normally the first appointment doesn't require an ultrasound."

"Doctor?" Margot turned her head. "Is that true?"

The doctor smiled at them both kindly. "Yes. Your partner really has done his research. But since you're further along in your pregnancy than most women normally are when they come in for their first appointment, I wanted to get an idea of what we're looking at. Development-wise, Miss Daley, your baby is in perfect health. Would you like to listen?"

"Listen?" Margot repeated curiously. "To what?"

The doctor's smile broadened. Before Eddie could parse all his recently acquired knowledge to know what she might mean, the doctor turned and adjusted something on her monitor. She kept the instrument she held pressed gently to Margot's stomach.

A hypnotic, rhythmic thrum filled the room. Eddie glanced from Margot to the speakers near them and back, and could tell that she was equally confused. "Is that...my heartbeat?" she asked.

"I'm using an advanced version of the fetal Doppler," the doctor explained. "Not every clinic has a setup like this." She indicated the speakers occupying each corner of the room. "It's a little dramatic, but I think it's appropriate for this moment. I don't just want expecting parents to hear their child's heartbeat; I want them to be able to *feel* it."

The steady pulse resonated in the room. As Eddie listened to it intently, holding his breath for any sort of irregularity, he found that the sound was starting to feel as if it came from *within* him. Was his own heart beating in time with the heartbeat of his child?

Was this how Margot felt at night, lying awake in bed alone, listening? He suddenly ached to be there with her in those moments.

"It's her." Margot looked at him, eyes shimmering. "It's our baby, Eddie."

"It's still too early at this stage to tell the sex," the doctor noted. Eddie knew that, but he didn't voice any doubts about Margot's certainty. He believed her statement as much as she appeared to believe it herself. *A daughter,* he thought in wonder. *My daughter.*

He reached for her, but Margot's hand was already moving off the table to seek his hand. They met halfway, interlocking their fingers; Eddie felt the warmth of their touch flow through him as their baby's heartbeat filled the room with its steady pulse. For the first time, he found himself trying to imagine all the lullabies he might sing to her. He hadn't conducted any research into the matter, and couldn't remember the words to the low refrains his own mother had once sung to him. Whatever he came up with, he knew that it would never inspire a similar feeling to what he felt in this moment. This was his own daughter's lullaby to *him.*

"And here you can see the baby on the screen," the doctor invited. Both their heads turned together to observe the sonogram. Eddie thought he had known what to expect, having browsed through galleries upon galleries of pictures online already, but his heart still gave a jolt when he saw the tiny figure tucked in close to itself. It was a similar sensation to seeing someone you thought you recognized after spending too long apart. He didn't know how else to describe it.

"Can we get a printout?" Margot sounded short of breath. Eddie glanced down at her quickly to make sure nothing was the matter, and saw that her expression was as awestruck as his own. He assumed that was the reason she struggled to form words now.

He squeezed her hand.

"Of course." The doctor smiled. "I've already ordered copies from the lab. Before you go, though, I did want to take a moment to talk with the two of you about Margot's blood pressure."

"Her blood pressure?" Eddie was already on high alert. "How is it? What's wrong?"

"Eddie," Margot murmured. "Let her finish."

"It's high." The doctor took a seat on the stool opposite from the two of them. She levelled a look at Margot that made Eddie feel immediately confirmed in his worry. "Much higher than I'd like it to be."

"Oh." Margot's eyebrows drew together in bewilderment. "That's strange. I've really been trying to take it easy recently."

You've been working even longer and harder hours than usual at the firm, Eddie corrected her privately, but he had the presence of mind to keep his thoughts to himself for the moment. He could discuss his concerns with Margot once they were alone.

"Wonderful," the doctor said. "I would advise you to step up your efforts even more. I'll have my nurse leave you with a list of activities you might consider pursuing – and staying away from." She rose to finish typing in one last note. "Overall I'm encouraged by our checkup, Miss Daley. The baby is healthy. That being said, do be sure to take steps to monitor your pressure and destress your life even more. I look forward to seeing you a few weeks from now."

"Understood," Margot cut in before Eddie could comment. She pulled her shirt down and maneuvered herself toward his side of the table; he was on his feet in an instant with a free hand to cradle her elbow, the other her waist. She slipped down to the floor and smiled up at him. "Ready to go?" she beamed.

Once they had collected their sonograms and confirmed the details of Margot's next appointment, they reconvened on the sidewalk outside of the clinic. They looked at one another.

"Wow," Margot said.

"Wow," Eddie agreed. "Is it just me, or is it all so…?"

"So much more real now?" she offered.

"I'm glad to hear you say it," he replied seriously. "Margot, I think we really need to take the doctor's instructions to heart. You're pushing yourself too hard, the same way you always have. It's not good for you, and it's not good for the baby."

Margot waved him off. "I'll be fine, Eddie. Really. I'm going with the flow of things, and that's exactly what the doctor prescribed. In fact, I bet my blood pressure is *better* than usual since I stopped worrying about what the future holds." She smiled, and Eddie couldn't resist reaching out to touch her hair. He had never looked at Margot as someone who was fragile before, but now he couldn't help it. It was like carrying his baby had reframed her, somehow, into someone more precious and breakable than he could have ever imagined the old Margot Daley being.

"I admire your new lease on life, Margot, especially after everything that's happened to us these past few months. Please don't think that I don't," he said. "But what if 'going with the flow' isn't enough? We have to plan these things out."

"Plan for the worst, you mean," she said. She drew back a little from his touch. "You don't think I can take care of myself on my own. Is that it?"

Eddie shook his head in exasperation. "That's not it. That's not it at all!" He wanted to shout his denial to the rooftops, but shouting was probably the last thing he needed to be doing right now. If Margot was going to accept her environment as it was, then Eddie was going to do his best to control for anything that might go wrong. Whether she knew it or not, he was going to make certain that she lived in a safe, comfortable bubble for the duration of this pregnancy. It's what a good man, a *responsible* man, was meant to do. And he was certain it's what her father would want to see.

Margot's eyes narrowed. "You know, Eddie, this controlling side of you is really starting to wear on me. It's like the moment I got pregnant you got it into your head that I'm completely help-less without you. I'm not. And I resent being treated like a child when I'm expecting a child of my own."

Margot might as well have pulled a whip out of her purse and administered thirty lashes, right then and there. Eddie actually felt the blood drain out of his face, as if it was rushing to some other part of his body that required attention… or as if it just didn't feel like sticking around to witness his humiliation.

65

For a moment, Margot looked as if she wanted to add something else. Eddie leaned forward, hoping for an opening to ingratiate himself once more—but she whirled on her heel and stalked down the sidewalk to hail a car. He didn't follow. After hearing her words, he knew better than to attempt to try. Margot wanted to be heard, not reconciled with.

As the cab pulled away, with her in it, Eddie was left standing on the curb alone to contemplate his options. He felt like he was constantly navigating a maze these days, coming up against wall after wall of outside expectations. Margot wanted him to go with the flow, but how could he? *This* was the test that had been placed before him, and he had to prove himself now more than ever. It was sink or swim for Eddie Jameson. It was time to finally earn the esteem of those closest to him by any means necessary.

And if that meant stepping in to guide Margot's flow, then he was prepared to do whatever was necessary to keep them both above water.

CHAPTER NINE

MARGOT

Margot never thought she'd say it, but she had liked "new Eddie" better when they were *actually* planning the wedding together. What had once seemed like a scary series of meetings to plan her future now seemed lighthearted, even *fun,* compared to the excessive worrying he spent all his time doing now.

"I swear, if he asks me about my blood pressure one more time…" she muttered to herself as she approached the door to his new apartment. Then again, maybe she wasn't just talking to herself. She touched her stomach, feeling as she so often did for the growing bump and the baby that lay beneath. She had mostly maintained her figure so far—probably owing to the fact that she could only keep down half of the food she ate anymore. Only her boobs seemed to have gotten significantly larger, and Margot wasn't complaining on that front. She was filling out her T-shirts and dresses in a way her slender frame had never allowed her to do before, and she could tell from the appreciative glances she was getting on the street that she looked good.

But there was only one pair of eyes she wanted looking at her that way. And it was the thought of seeing them again that kept drawing her back in. All it had taken was a text of invitation from Eddie to get her out the door. She could endure his poking and prodding, she decided, if he would just keep looking at her like he had in recent days.

It was a beautiful evening in New York; warm, almost muggy. She thought she had arrived at the right address in the complex, but checked her texts from Eddie to be sure. She had only ever visited him at his brownstone before. When she was satisfied that she had the right place—and after checking her lipstick off the reflection in her phone—Margot breathed in a deep breath and knocked on the door.

Eddie pulled it open almost as soon as she had retracted her fist. Margot blinked rapidly in surprise. He looked...not at all how she had expected him to look. His auburn hair was damp and slicked-back, and he was wearing a white fluffy robe. Had he really just gotten out of the shower this late in the evening? Had he forgotten she was coming over? *He* was the one who had extended the invitation! Maybe some of the old Eddie still existed beneath this new responsible exterior after all. She didn't know whether to run for the hills or breathe a much-needed sigh of relief.

"How's your blood pressure?" His handsome face hovered so close she thought he would kiss her hello, and was sorely disappointed when he didn't. "Did you find the place okay? Want to sit down?"

"I'm fine." Margot brushed past him, keeping her wrists out of the way of his hands. He had made it a habit in recent days of seizing hold of her and checking her pulse against his watch, the way the doctor had taught him, and she didn't want him to alarm himself needlessly. Her heart always beat too rapidly when he was around. "This new place is amazing! What happened to the brownstone?"

"I'm renting both to test things out. I always wanted a bit more space." Eddie crossed his arms, something he usually did when he wanted to emphasize his biceps, but the robe made him look like a benevolent wizard. Margot's eyebrows shot up at his answer, and he gestured for her to continue into the apartment. "Come on! I'll give you the tour."

Margot followed him down the hallway, running her fingers along the walls and stopping to peer into rooms. "Wow, Eddie, this layout is incredible! There's enough space here to fit three families. You really scored with this one."

"I thought you might like it." Eddie was beside her shoulder, an over-attentive, fluffy white guardian angel. He certainly looked as if he could fly off the balcony in those sleeves. Margot turned, and was surprised when she bumped into him. His robe fell open a little, and her hands came up to brace themselves against the pie slice of chest their collision exposed. Eddie grunted with surprise, and brought his own hands up to stabilize her shoulders.

God, his pecs were out of this world. She didn't move her hands from their fixed position, but allowed her fingers to linger along the tight swell of muscle, reveling in her memories of what they had felt like flexing as he surged atop her. Her face warmed, and she had a feeling she was blushing. Margot's father hadn't raised her to be a crier, and he certainly hadn't raised her to be a blusher, but she seemed to be doing a lot of both recently in the privacy of her own apartment. She was pretty sure hormones were to blame. She certainly blamed them for her body's response to Eddie now.

She hadn't accepted his invitation with any expectation of becoming...intimate. Sometimes, standing back to watch Eddie schedule every appointment and take charge of their to-do lists, Margot had a sinking feeling thoughts of sex were the furthest thing from his mind. Maybe *she* was the dirty pervert now, always privately replaying the steamier moments of their one-night stand and aching for a repeat. She couldn't get too near him most days without feeling flushed beneath the collar and between the legs.

Except when he insisted on taking her blood pressure.

"Sorry. I really do want to give you space if you need it. Now, and...at other times." His hands, so warm and strong-fingered, ran up and down her shoulders. The gentle friction shouldn't have been enough to excite her, but it was.

"I don't want space from you." Margot flushed at her own words, before recovering enough to offer him a little half-smile that was several degrees cooler than the rest of her. "But isn't this just a tad bit more expensive than what you're used to paying?" She was only poking fun at him, of course. If she was turning into the filthy-minded one, then Eddie Jameson was at least as equally filthy rich. She was surprised he had kept the brownstone for so long already, considering he had spent the last few years traveling to the next exotic locale. She wondered if anchoring himself to a new apartment, and a new situation, scared him at all.

Eddie grinned down at her. "I think I can afford it."

She returned his smile with a teasing one of her own. "Guess you're right. My dad *is* one of your clients, after all."

She leaned in for a kiss, but pulled up short. Eddie's expression was odd in the aftermath of her remark. It wasn't the first time she had teased him about their families' business connection, but he looked as stunned now as if she had slapped him. Before she could puzzle over what his look meant, and decide whether or not to apologize for crossing some unknown line, Eddie sighed and passed a hand over his face. When he returned to her, he was smiling once more.

"Come on. Come check out the private roof deck. But before you do—" Eddie crossed to the kitchen table. He pulled an identical white robe from the back of a chair and tossed it to her with a grin. Margot caught it

"Matching outfits already?" she joked. "I thought we had a decade at *least* before we reached that point."

"I'm a fast mover." Eddie's smile broadened, and Margot's heart sped yet again at the sight of his Adonis-like features beaming down on her. What the heck was with her recently? This was *Eddie Jameson,* the kid she had known since diapers, the exasperating guy she had seen stumble awkwardly through his teenage years and come out on the other side accidently looking like a yachting magazine model. He wasn't some gorgeous stranger worth getting star-struck over!

"You certainly weren't a fast mover when it came to me," she mused.

"Are you referring to how long I last in the bedroom?" Eddie schooled his expression, as if they were discussing something as mundane as the meeting minutes. Margot smothered an answering giggle with her hand. *Get a grip, Margot.* She was so *not* the type of girl to usually be charmed by innuendo, especially not when it was such low-hanging fruit for a clever guy like Eddie, but she couldn't help it. He had a way of making her feel like a teenager again...

So long as he didn't bring up the wedding. Or her doctor's appointments. Or her blood pressure.

"Here. Check it out." He invited her into the kitchen, and Margot followed. "I've got everything set up for a relaxing night in."

He wasn't joking. He had already filled two steaming ceramic tea bowls with what smelled like authentic green tea. There was a beautiful crystalline pitcher of ice water sweating beside a pyramid of warm, rolled towels. "I was almost expecting a blood pressure cuff," she joked as Eddie handed her one of the mugs of tea. "What is all this?"

"I told you already. But if you're curious about the robe, put it on, and I'll show you."

Margot raised an eyebrow. "Is that the gentleman's way of asking me to strip?"

Eddie's cheeks colored beneath his tan. She had always known what buttons to push to make the infamous Blush-Inducer himself heat up. "I mean...nice as that outfit is," he punctuated his compliment with an approving look, "you're going to have to get out of those clothes somehow if you want to see what I have planned. If you want me to stick around..."

Of all the nights to corner him! Margot wanted nothing more than to put on her favorite R&B mix and show him the sultry moves she had been too wasted and horny to properly execute the first time. In fact, if memory served, Eddie had been the one to tear away her clothes in an impatient whirlwind the last time they found themselves in this promising position.

But Margot couldn't bring herself to be bold now, and she hated herself for it. She fingered the soft fabric of the robe as she tried to summon from the reserve of courage she usually had in surplus. Looks like she had spent it all on wedding planning and baby logistics. No way Eddie would look at her the way he was looking at her now the moment she removed her clothes and he saw her changing body. Her boobs may look killer, but she was all too aware that she was beginning to get extra padding else- where. *Maybe* she could pull off not looking totally pregnant if she wore the right things, but for how much longer?

It was probably safer to err on the side of being a prude.

Margot offered him her best crooked smile. "Somehow I don't think *Zelma* would approve," she said.

Eddie chuckled. "You know I think she wanted to take a bite out of me? I can't decide if it was in a good way. Anyway, in honor of our favorite changing room chaperones, I will demur."

"As will I." She waited until Eddie's back was turned to let her disappointed look out of the cage. She reminded herself that this was the right decision. There might have been a time when she wanted Eddie Jameson to see her naked, but it wasn't now. As soon as she felt certain he wouldn't peek, Margot shimmied out of her clothes and engulfed herself in the robe. It was hard to feel too badly when you were wearing something that felt like it could have been fashioned from a cloud captured above some distant, exotic coast. She breathed in the smell of fabric softened appreciatively as Eddie led her outside.

"Oh, *Eddie.*"

She was surprised she could get even those two simple words out. The view from the apartment's rooftop was the most fantastic she had ever seen – and as an architect, Margot had stood on a *lot* of New York rooftops. There were no neighboring complexes as tall as theirs, and she could see all the way out to the velvet blue of New York Harbor unobstructed. The Statue of Liberty arose on its island, bright green against the backdrop and in defiant miniature at a distance. Above them, the evening sky was a gorgeous cobalt gradient without a single cloud obstructing its face. At her feet, candles. Eddie had arranged twenty, thirty...maybe *fifty* candles, all perched on tiny white saucers, and not a single one had snuffed itself out. Margot gazed around herself at the flickering field of fire. *This is so not up to code,* she thought. She raised her hands to her mouth to hide her expanding, elated smile at the sight.

"I paid extra for the unit with private rooftop access," Eddie mentioned. His eyes shone as he watched her.

"Eddie, this is incredible," she enthused. "All of it."

"*And* there's a full moon tonight," Eddie mentioned. As if the bright, silver sphere lording over it all wasn't the least bit self-evident. Margot did laugh then. She wanted to spin around beneath it with her head thrown to the sky, like she had back when they were kids. *You know what? Fuck it.* She flung her arms wide and turned in place, as if she hoped to fit the entire, incredible view in an embrace.

"Eddie, this is amazing," she said seriously.

"I did good?" He looked at her like a puppy dog awaiting a treat to prove it, but there was a spark of self-aware humor in his eyes.

"You did good," she assured. When she found she couldn't easily pull her gaze from his, she managed to break off by nodding toward the yoga mats. "I didn't exactly come dressed for...whatever it is you have in store."

"That's the great thing about naked yoga," Eddie said as he shrugged out of his robe. "No dress code."

Oh my God. Margot tried not to let her jaw too obviously drop as Eddie sprang not one, but two, very *big* surprises on her in the same instant. In all honesty, she probably should have seen this coming. *Of course* Eddie would be into naked yoga. What did she think the robe was for? She supposed she had been expecting something like an intimate couples' massage, but this...this...

This involved Eddie Jameson. Naked. Standing in front of her. She shouldn't have been shocked by it, considering that clothes hadn't exactly been an active ingredient when it came to conceiving this surprise pregnancy. Still, her night with Eddie had been a lust-fueled, alcohol-laden blur – by the end of it, she had been barely able to remember where her body began and his ended, which meant that she hadn't exactly paused to get a proper eyeful of him.

Eddie's body was standing before her in crystal-clear definition now. Everything, from his shoulders to his pecs to his calves, was corded in rock-hard muscle. He was even fitter than she had imagined him being, considering he had always proudly boasted of staying out of the gym. All that sailing really kept him in great shape.

Margot's eyes dragged downward to take in the view below his Adonis belt. She was less surprised to find that Eddie was as well-hung as she remembered. Maybe he wasn't erect now, but he certainly had plenty to work with...and work it he did. Her chest and neck heated with the recollection.

Was it her imagination, or did his cock twitch slightly beneath her gaze? She realized suddenly that she had let her robe slip down over one shoulder while she was drinking him in. Margot grimaced, and quickly pulled it back up.

Eddie gasped with faux shock. "Margot, I'm surprised at you. You're going to make me do naked yoga *alone?*"

"I..." She couldn't come up with an adequate defense. She dropped her eyes sheepishly and settled for something close to the truth. "I don't know, Eddie. I'm not the young filly I once was." *Oh God, Margot, did you really just say that?* Her wince deepened, but she couldn't take back the embarassing excuse now.

Eddie laughed. "Margie, what the hell are you talking about? You're twenty-eight, living in *New York City,* and you're the most gorgeous thing in any room you walk into! What do you mean you aren't 'young'? That's got to be the oldest thing I've ever heard you say!"

"I mean I'm getting fat, Eddie," Margot grumbled. "There, I said it."

Eddie's eyes descended to take her in. "You're crazy," he said, and she could tell by his tone that he thought he was being completely honest. "Margot, have you seen yourself recently? You look sensational."

"But for how much longer?" She crossed her arms over her chest. She didn't want to double-down on her own idiotic bout of self-consciousness, but when he looked at her like that...and said the exact right charming things to her...she knew she was in danger of caving.

And would Eddie be singing the same complimentary tune once she let the robe drop?

He crossed the yoga mat to her. Margot fought the urge to turn from him. She held her ground, and let him settle his hands on her shoulders. "Look, if it makes you feel any better, I've done my research," Eddie mentioned.

"Not this again," Margot moaned.

He held up a hand. "Hear me out. Yoga is a great way to keep your stress in check, and keep your blood pressure down. Not only that, but it's a low-impact exercise, so it will help you keep that hot body of yours looking - and feeling – healthy and beautiful. Naked yoga just happens to be my favorite. And if it didn't already bear that distinction before tonight..." Eddie's eyes climbed her again, lingering for a long moment on the open collar of her robe. "...the fact that I get to do it naked with you makes it my favorite thing on earth. But only if you're comfortable," he added.

"Do you do this all the time?" Margot asked hesitantly. When Eddie nodded, her eyes narrowed. "With other women?"

"By myself," he admitted. "And I was introduced to it once at a work retreat...not that my brothers knew where it was exactly I had snuck off to." Eddie grinned. "But you're the first person I've welcomed into my personal practice. Namaste, Margot."

"Namaste, Eddie," she returned with a little smile. She knew he had successfully sweet-talked her; still, she couldn't bring her fingers to undo the cord around her waist and begin. Eddie, seeing her hesitation, seemed to sense what was needed. His hands came around her waist slowly, and he slipped the knot open.

The heavy robe fell from her shoulders and pooled at her feet. The candlelight flickered across her bare skin the same way it licked along his. Eddie's hands smoothed up her shoulders, warming her goosebumps, and then slid down her forearms. He wouldn't bring himself to touch anything else, although he stared at her breasts openly, almost hungrily. Margot was surprised when she didn't feel shy beneath the intensity of his look; she felt invigorated.

"Shall we start with breathing?" Eddie's voice sounded strained, as if his lungs weren't quite functioning properly.

"That may be a good idea," she whispered.

"All right. Six deep breaths," he murmured. "Follow my lead."

Margot skimmed her hands along his chest. She watched, fascinated, as the muscles seemed to rise beneath her touch...as if she was the energy that inspired him to breathe. She breathed in the night air along with him, and expelled it in a sigh. She closed her eyes. As she pressed her hand to Eddie's chest, she felt one of his own hands come up to touch hers. He held it over her heart.

"Breathe," he repeated. Margot breathed.

Eddie's touch caressed lower. Her nipple, already tight from the kiss of the cool breeze, strained towards his hand. Just when she thought he would tease her by maintaining a light touch, Eddie palmed her breast and squeezed.

With her next breath, Margot sighed.

"Breathe," he said again. His voice was much closer to her this time. When her eyes fluttered open, she discovered Eddie's face mere inches from her own. "Breathe." He caught her shallow outtake of breath as he leaned in and kissed her.

Margot melted in his arms. More and more recently, she had been wanting him to kiss her like this. She almost couldn't concentrate during their encounters without first tasting the reprieve of his lips; they were too distracting in the way that they formed words, relayed *research...*when all she really wanted was for them to be on her. All of her. It was the only language she had found so far that could articulate how she felt around him, and Eddie spoke it in spades.

His tongue wound with hers in a sensuous dance. Margot thought the candle flames had leapt into their mouths, the way they undulated and joined together. Every breath she took, Eddie also took, gasping it into himself. She was pretty sure this wasn't the proper technique to assume when it came to yoga breathing. Her pulse beat wildly and resounded in her like a drum. She swore she could feel the heat of the fire surrounding them: every tiny pinprick suddenly joined together in her peripheral to rage like an inferno. Eddie's touch, his kiss, were the things stoking the blaze.

And Margot couldn't have cared less anymore about the fire code.

Eddie crossed his legs and drew her down with him. Margot

followed, helpless to resist the pull of his dark eyes. God, she could lose herself in the way he looked at her. Eddie had always been capable of speaking unvoiced volumes in the span of a single glance; his face was an open book to anyone he chose to let read it, and there was something completely irresistible about a natural charmer like him selecting *her* as the sole focus of his attention. Margot had always felt that way, whether they found themselves coming together inside a crowded room, or alone and fumbling around in the dark back at his brownstone. Eddie knew how to make her feel like she was the most special person in the world to him. No one else's opinion of her mattered as much as his did, save her own opinion of herself. With Eddie, she was safe and looked-after. She could let herself go completely.

His erection jutted proudly between his legs, nestled in a bushel of neatly-groomed curls. Margot sat astride it, never quite lowering her full weight onto him; she maintained enough space between them to give her fingers full license to run along Eddie's treasure trail. He hissed a pleasured purr at her fleeting caresses. His cock slotted itself between her legs, and she rocked herself on it, enjoying the little thrills that shot through her every time her hips undulated forward and brought her clit into contact with his pelvis. Her hands smoothed up his chest, and she wrapped her arms around his neck. Eddie gripped her waist, lightly pushing and pulling her against him in tandem with her thrusts.

She met his lips hungrily with her own. Eddie's kiss was hot and slick and deep; she had always guessed he would be a good kisser. He *had* been her first kiss, once upon a time, but the chaste pecks they had shared when they were children were nothing compared to the kind of kisses he lavished on her now.

One, two, three sweeps and he massaged her mouth open; Margot made a breathless noise as his tongue swept past her teeth and tangled with her own. The kiss didn't endure nearly long enough to satisfy her. Almost as soon as he had memorized the taste of her, Eddie pulled back to tongue the hollow of her neck. Just as she was starting to enjoy *that*, he dragged his face up to nip at her chin with the edges of his teeth.

It was like their first night together all over again. Lately there had been so much emphasis on the wedding, and the baby, that Margot had almost feared what intimacy with Eddie would be like. What if it wasn't as good as she remembered? What if they weren't the slightest bit physically compatible, *at all?* But maybe, just maybe, it hadn't been the alcohol that had blurred her better judgement that time and caused her every sense to converge into one. Maybe it had been Eddie all along, the strength of her feelings for him, and his answering passion.

Maybe they were better together than she could have ever believed possible.

His erection strained beneath her, and his hips rose in small, questing thrusts that were becoming more and more frequent. She felt a hand fish between her legs to rub and finger and tease. She gasped and arched in his arms, and kissed every inch of his face that came within reach of her frantic lips. She mouthed the hard curve of his jaw; she let her lips drag along one rough cheek, relishing the lingering spearmint taste of his aftershave; she worshipped his temple and licked the shell of his ear. He groaned, as if her every ministration drove him closer and closer to an unseen breaking point. His fingers answered her by rubbing harder along her outer folds. He sank one into her, and when he found her already damp with anticipation, slid another in beside it. Margot rocked into the sensation, driving Eddie's fingers several joints deeper, and gave a little cry when he struck that secret node that could make the world come apart at its seams.

"Margot..." Eddie's voice was deeper than she remembered it being several seconds before. She kept kissing him fervently; she wanted to see just how husky it could get when saying her name. Eddie groaned and extracted his fingers. She tensed as he pushed her thighs wide, then...

Margot sank down onto his cock with a moan that almost sounded like a sigh of relief. She let her head fall back, and closed her eyes against even the breathtaking view of the skyline; everything she wanted in that moment was in her arms, and she wanted to experience Eddie to the utmost. She lost herself completely in the sensation of joining with him again. How had they ever let themselves be parted before?

"Feel good?" Eddie's voice was low and coaxing, but there was a spark of the old deviousness there that she had been missing so much these past months. The fact that it would reappear now was almost too erotic for words. It was like Eddie was some kind of sensual shape-changer whose true nature was only revealed to her now that they were out in the open air, beneath the city lights and the glowing face of the moon.

Once she had settled fully in his lap, and acclimated herself to how well he filled her, Margot began to move. She no longer felt held back by her apprehensions about their relationship, or how she looked, or what the next day would bring. A metamorphosis didn't have to be a scary thing; with Eddie, she could spread new wings and take flight. As she rocked against him, she reveled in the way her heavier breasts bounced against her rib cage. This new body was *sensational.* How had she not paused to appreciate it before?

Eddie's fingers inched up her stomach, and Margot smiled to herself. She pressed a hand to his chest and pushed him down; he fell backward into the yoga mat, and she rearranged her hips around his pelvis. Now that he was lying sprawled beneath her, he had better access to her breasts. His hands were on her again almost before she had time to adjust to their new position.

"Holy shit Margot," he breathed. "You look *incredible.*"

She leaned down as if to whisper a secret. "I feel incredible, Eddie." Her words stirred a loose strand of hair that had fallen forward into her face, and she didn't bother blowing it back. She was sultry; powerful. Every part of her in disarray was natural and beautiful, and she wanted Eddie to stamp this moment in his memory. She cupped his face in her hands as she began to move against him once more. "I feel incredible when I'm with you," she said.

"I feel the same."

His broad hands squeezed her breasts, then gave them an experimental roll. Margot bit her lip. She couldn't help smiling at the incredulous look on Eddie's face as he took her in. He pinched her left nipple and glanced up to gauge her reaction. Margot's hips bucked, almost without her consent, and she hissed as he pulled the rosebud taut. "That feel good?" Eddie asked.

"Stop checking in with me," Margot growled. She didn't want to feel like she was being looked after, not right now. She jerked her hips clockwise, and Eddie's hands fell away. His head rocked back and hit the yoga mat.

"Fuck!"

More like it. Margot drew her lip back between her teeth and gave him her best pair of temptress eyes. She lowered her lashes and swirled her hips again.

"Oh, *fuck,*" Eddie moaned. "Don't look at me like that."

"Like what?" Margot arched her back and raised her ass up off him. It wasn't quite enough height to make Eddie withdraw from her fully, but almost. She kept the thick tip of his cock buried inside her, just enough to tease them both. "How am I looking at you? And what happens if I keep doing it?"

"God," Eddie groaned. The hands on her hips tried to pull her back down to engulf him, but she resisted; she wiggled a little instead, and was rewarded with a noise she had never heard him make before. "I really met my match in you, didn't I?"

"Took you long enough to realize." Margot was pleased with his remark. She decided to reward them both by easing herself back down over his shaft. Eddie seized beneath her, and his head fell back again; her moan joined in with his as she settled down atop him once more. "So what yoga poses did you want to show me?" she panted. She doubted she would be able to successfully control her breathing at all with him buried so far inside her, but she was willing to keep up the pretense of "couples yoga" for at least a few minutes more. She enjoyed teasing Eddie way too much to give up and go at it this early...even though the way he moved beneath her made it sorely tempting.

"Well..." Eddie paused as she thrust herself forward a little atop him, and continued when she decided to relent and allow him to speak, "...I was thinking we could start slow with something basic, like..."

84

Margot cried out in delight as he bucked up beneath her. He propped himself on his forearms, clenched his ass muscles, and lifted his hips; she clung on and rode every up and down movement, tightening her knees and hiking her legs up on either side of his waist. His pelvic thrusts were strong, controlled, and uninterrupted. It was as if her weight atop him meant nothing, and she marveled at how easy he made it look...but it was hard to concentrate on something as G-rated as Eddie's form when he was busy pumping himself inside her. She cried out and planted her hands on his chest. His skin was already slick with sweat from their exertions, and it would only be harder to find purchase as they proceeded.

But Margot was up for the challenge.

"Are you...familiar...with this one?" Eddie's eyes were so dark they had to be all pupil as he watched her ride him. The flames off the candles surrounding them glimmered in the depths of his gaze.

The same strand of errant hair fell into her eyes as she bounced. Margot blew a defiant gust of breath to push it back. Her hands were tasked with keeping herself balanced atop the surging body beneath her. "I'm familiar." She bit the words out quickly before their jouncing drew another moan. "What else you got?"

"I don't know if you can handle it."

Margot scoffed at his cockiness. When Eddie next lowered himself to the mat, she planted her knees and moved her body in a series of feline undulations. "Why don't you show me, hot-shot?"

"I'd love to."

Eddie surged forward, seizing hold of her thighs to keep them tightly wrapped around him as he upended her. It was the same strength of his arms that she had been admiring that kept her from falling backward on her ass now. She cried out in momentary protest, so sure the maneuver would cause his cock to slip free from her and put an abrupt pause to intercourse, but his hips followed hers closely. He laid her down and shoved his hands along the insides of her legs, coaxing them up over his shoulders. Margot arched and hissed as she eased into the stretch. Thankfully, she kept herself warmed-up and flexible most days...an intimate detail that Eddie was privy to since their first night together. She still remembered the look that had crossed his face when he realized the possibilities her own athleticism brought to the bedroom. He had certainly tried to get her into every possible position he could at the time.

They had both thought it was a one-night fling, after all. They had made drunken love that first go-around like they were running out of time.

Now, Eddie seemed intent on learning every inch of her at his own excruciating pace. His hands trailed up her legs, wicking perspiration. Margot moaned and trembled beneath him. She loved the searing burn of her muscles at work, locking into their new position hooked around his shoulders. Eddie circled her ankles with his fingers and clenched, holding her firmly in place. He started to surge forward into her again, and Margot raised her hips up off the mat to better accommodate their new position. The slap of flesh rang louder, increasing in frequency as Eddie started to lose the last vestiges of his control.

"Eddie..." Her own cry of pleasure cut her off. She wasn't

even sure what she had been about to say. Maybe she'd only been gearing up to beg him aloud for what her body already told him it wanted.

Eddie pumped into her harder, faster, with an answering groan that sounded like he had intended for it to be a real response. His cock felt so rigid and unrelenting thrusting inside her that Margot couldn't remember a world without it. Her focus had narrowed to that single, overactive point where their fevered bodies joined; her hips moved to meet him as if someone else was pulling them on a string. She didn't have to worry anymore, or plan, or even think. Her body was on blissful autopilot, putting her through the necessary motions that would lead her to that ultimate...

"Ah! Oh, God, Eddie! I'm coming!"

Margot froze and reached for him, and Eddie gave her himself to hold onto. He let go of her legs so they could fall and wrap around his waist; she hooked her ankles and clenched as he buried himself deeply inside her. He craned forward, pushing their chests together, sealing her cries with the hot, wet press of his mouth. It was the sensation of his lips that put her over the edge. Margot returned his kiss with a passion that should have burned them both up as she came in a burst of incendiary pleasure. Orgasm rolled through her in warm, cresting waves; her thoughts fragmented and were pulled out to sea. She sank back into complete bliss.

Distantly, she felt Eddie shudder on top of her. She threaded her fingers through the hair at the nape of his neck and pulled him in close as he came; she laved her tongue along the hot seam of his lips until he opened it, groaning, and let her slip inside. He spent himself between her thighs and collapsed heavily atop her.

Margot stroked his forehead, enjoying the feel of him resting in her arms. After a moment, he lifted his head. His rich auburn hair hung forward in his eyes, damp with sweat. He gave an exhausted chuckle as his eyes fell on her. Eddie gazed with such feeling that it shook Margot more deeply than any mind-blowing orgasm she could experience at his expert hands. She lifted her hand to smooth his hair back tenderly, and smiled.

"So. How about that iced tea, Miss Daley?" he suggested.

"That sounds delightful. Thank you, Eddie." Margot laughed. "Are you ever under-prepared, Mr. Jameson?"

Eddie withdrew and rolled off her. She lay basking in the afterglow of terrific sex, soaking in the bright rays of the moon. She felt like a goddess who had just been *thoroughly* worshipped and found her tribute more than satisfactory.

"Never, with the exception of last time." Eddie grinned.

"You mean that time I got you drunk and rode you bare-back?" she inquired. "I admit it rings a bell. Why, do you regret letting me have my wicked, unprotected way with you?"

Eddie settled a hand on the smooth plane of her stomach. His unexpected touch surprised her; after a moment, Margot laid her hand tentatively upon his. She wondered if he could feel two pulses beating in time.

"I don't regret a thing," Eddie said. He withdrew his hand and rose before she could come up with a response. "You wait right here. Don't budge even an inch. I meant it when I said I wanted you to have a relaxing night in...even if the last twenty minutes might not make that totally apparent." He treated her to his signature crooked grin, and turned to go inside. Despite his command for total immobilization, Margot propped herself up on her elbow to watch him. She loved the way the moonlight pooled along his naked muscles as he moved, filling in every hard hollow of him like liquid silver. If Eddie thought they would be relaxing tonight, then he was sorely mistaken.

Margot was already ready for round two.

CHAPTER TEN

EDDIE

"Hey Eddie." Margot bounced across the top deck of *Annabella* and over to where he stood pouring her a glass of sparkling cider, and draped her arms around his shoulders. "What's the wireless password?"

Eddie had already seen this coming a mile away. After a stressful week at work - not to mention a stressful week of rushing to plan out every detail of the wedding - he could see that Margot was wearing thin. Despite showing no signs of stopping, and despite the puppy dog eyes she was making at him now, he knew her too well. Her blood pressure was probably sky-high, even if she wouldn't let him close enough to get a cuff on her and check for certain.

That was precisely why he had invited her to spend the night aboard *Annabella* with him. It was the end of the week, and there was no better way for the hard-working mother of his child to spend a Friday night than relaxing with him to tend to her every need.

And that meant absolutely no contact with the frenetics of the outside world.

"There isn't a password," he replied. "I deactivated the Internet. No browsing for fun, and definitely no working while we're onboard."

"Ugh." Margot pouted, but she didn't extract her arms from around him like he'd expected her to. "You're really taking the doctor's words as a health scare, aren't you? Not that I can truly complain about being doted on." She whisked the glass of cider out of his hand, threw her beautiful head back–and downed it in one single, sensuous swallow. She batted her eyes and held it out again expectantly, and Eddie felt certain she was trying to send him some sort of signal...but he was determined it was the only signal either of them were going to get access to tonight. If Margot wanted to check her work e-mail, she would have to do it over his Wifi-withholding, sober-in-solidarity body.

"Look, we both could use a breather," he explained. "I know you've been going hard at work. I don't need to call your secretary or otherwise spy on you to guess that you haven't slowed your roll. It isn't who you are."

"Thank you," Margot said primly as she accepted his offered refill. "For what I'm taking as a compliment."

"It was meant as a compliment," he insisted. "And anyway, William's been riding my ass at work all week. I thought we deserved the evening off to escape." In truth, the project that William was so relentlessly demanding Eddie's attention on was the most recent Daley Flights ad campaign launch. William's idea of perfection could be even more inflexible than Sam's if the right ingredients–and the right clients–were involved, and Eddie could only keep so many balls in the air. Between the baby, the wedding plans, the launch specs...and trying to keep his brothers, clients, fiancée, and fiancée's family happy...he feared he was headed for a potential disaster. Better to back away for twenty-four hours and tackle it all again when he could see straight and mitigate the chaos.

Because of course he could *handle* it. He was Eddie Jameson. The people in his life were finally starting to respect him, to rely on him. He just hadn't expected them to all demand his attention at once.

"You don't want anyone riding your ass this evening. Got it." Margot retreated from him to lounge once more on one of the outdoor recliners. She took her time crossing her legs, and Eddie's cock lurched when he saw what she meant for him to see. Beneath that innocent yellow sundress, she wasn't wearing any underwear.

Any thought he had entertained of a relaxing evening with Margot quickly fled. Eddie set his own glass of cider aside and crossed to her. She watched him through her lashes, holding a quizzical expression until the last minute. By the time he had scooped her up in his arms, she was shrieking and flailing and laughing girlishly. She hung her own arms around his neck as he carried her below.

Eddie hadn't planned to make love to Margot so early in the evening. He had been strict with himself when working out a potential schedule for intimacy, and it wasn't something he had expected to initiate–but how could he resist her when she looked as delicious as the too-sweet cider they had quenched themselves on already?

"Come here." He growled low and primal in his throat as he laid her down on the bed. Margot giggled again and kicked her legs; he caught one calf and slipped her shoe off before she could tease him by pulling it out of reach. Another little kick sent her other shoe flying off her toe into a far corner of the *Annabella's* bedroom.

He considered helping her shed her sundress, but that thought flew entirely from his mind the moment she pulled him down for a deep, sensuous kiss. Eddie nipped and lapped at her lips until she parted them, and he tasted the sweet nectar of the cider they had shared above deck. His hand delved beneath the skirt of her dress. He stroked the hot, soft flesh hidden between her legs, and swallowed the pleasured purr she gave at his most intimate touch. When he hooked a finger along her entrance and thrust it experimentally inside her, her back arched, and her hips raised up off the mattress to meet him.

"I'll come," she gasped as she drew him down again. "For you, I'll come."

Eddie hiked the soft petals of her dress up around her waist as her fingers quickly wrestled the front of his pants open. Her haste to free him was as massive a turn-on as the brief glimpse of herself she had given him earlier; by the time his cock sprang into her eager hands, he was already hard as a rock.

"Mmm," Margot hummed appreciatively against her lips. She pulled Eddie toward her by the hips and lowered her mouth to lavish attention along his length. Eddie groaned, thrusting into the eager wet heat of her mouth, and she wrapped her lips around him. She pumped a hand along his base as she sucked him, and his next groan was explosive. He had to brace his hands against her shoulders to get her to stop before she undid him completely.

Margot raised her hazel eyes to him in loving invitation, and Eddie laid her back down, cradling her head as he eased her back into the pillow. He buried himself in the sweet scent of her neck as her hands found him and guided him home.

He slipped his cock inside her, letting her secret warmth engulf him utterly. She was ready to receive him, as slick as she was tight, and she hissed with pleasure as he angled his hips and struck that sweet hidden spot inside her. "More," he thought he heard her pant, but he couldn't be sure. He was so lost in the sensation of her that he was beyond comprehending anything else. Every muscle, every fiber of his being, sang with awareness of how perfectly she fit him – and how perfectly he filled her.

"Margot." He groaned her name as he surged against her. She lifted her legs off the bed and wrapped them around his pumping waist. His abdominals brushed against her soft belly. Every feminine curve of her drove him wild; his hands roamed along her every dip, swell, and plunge, memorizing the contours of her body, reveling at the way she had changed and would continue to change. Yet she was still *Margot,* the girl he had adored since childhood, the mother of his child, the woman that was to be his wife. Thinking of her in every precious context now was enough to put him over the edge. Several more thrusts and Eddie spilled himself inside her, losing himself completely in the wet, heavenly sensation between her legs. He collapsed atop her with a sated groan. After several moments, he managed to summon his remaining strength to overturn himself beside her.

"Mmm." Margot snuggled close, and Eddie wrapped his arm protectively around her shoulders. Her curves may have been filling out, but she still felt so petite in his arms. He didn't know if it was a natural conclusion to come to when he compared Margot's size to his own, or if he was only more aware of how precious she was to him now than he had been before. "This is nice," she murmured.

"Nowhere on earth I'd rather be right now," he agreed.

"Interesting, considering we aren't technically *on* solid ground at the moment." Margot sat up a little to look at him. A wave of tenderness washed over Eddie. He reached up to tuck a sex-disheveled piece of hair back behind one of her adorable ears.

"You could say that again," he murmured. "I haven't felt like there was solid ground beneath me since I saw you that night. Our first."

"It's been the same for me." Margot pillowed her cheek against her fist as she looked at him. "Eddie, do you know what my dream wedding would really be?" she inquired.

Eddie drew her down deeper into his arms. "Tell me," he whispered.

"My dream wedding, my *perfect* wedding, would be just the three of us, adrift out at sea." Margot sighed, and as she spoke, the images washed over him. "It would be so romantic to just say goodbye to everything and everyone we knew."

"The three of us," Eddie murmured.

"You, me, and the baby. We'd leave New York behind us for a little while," Margot said. "Just for a little while. And then we'd come back, a conquering family, and surprise all our friends and acquaintances and *clients*. Wouldn't that be something?"

Eddie squeezed her in answer. He could feel himself already starting to drift into the easiest sleep he'd had in a while, comforted by the lullaby of the future she spun for them. He didn't care whether or not he dreamed tonight: it was a dream enough already to have Margot here with him in his arms.

Annabella hummed beneath him. Eddie stirred and blinked the sleep from his eyes. He was lying in his favorite pool of cool, satin sheets, in a shaft of sunlight that strobed occasionally as the boat rocked. He yawned and stretched his arms. He groped around for Margot to pull her closer, and came up short.

That's when it hit him: not only was Margot missing. His boat was moving.

Someone was driving *Annabella* without him.

"Margot!" Her name slipped from his lips in a shout. Eddie rolled out of bed and quite literally hit the deck; he struggled upstairs, dragging the sheet with him as an afterthought. He was in a blind panic thinking his boat was stolen...thinking that someone had boarded while he slept and gotten hold of Margot, or the baby...he had forgotten to mop last night. What if she put her foot down wrong and slipped on a puddle of water? What if she tumbled overboard?

His fears were like a runaway train with an endless number of cars in tow, but as soon as he surfaced from below deck, he breathed a temporary sigh of relief. It was Margot behind the wheel; he could see her curvaceous silhouette posted up and steering *Annabella* with an easy, expert hand.

Then he woke fully, and the reality of the situation registered with him. Margot, pregnant with his child, was piloting his boat – no easy, or relaxing, feat. Eddie shouldered his way onto the deck and crossed to her quickly.

"Margot," he repeated, voice a bit more even this time; at the very least he wasn't shouting in a blind panic. "What the hell is going on? Where are we? How long have you been out here alone like this?"

"Relax, Eddie!" she laughed as she stepped back to let him take over at the wheel. "I'm not going to crash it. I've been driving my father's boat since I was five years old."

"You shouldn't be driving anything at all!" he exclaimed. He didn't care if he sounded like a raving lunatic; he didn't care if he *looked* like one, barely wearing a sheet like he had just woken after an all-night toga party. He had one hand on the wheel, and one holding his makeshift garment up to conceal himself from any other boats they might pass out on the harbor. "This is exactly what the doctor warned us against doing right now."

"I thought I would surprise you." Margot's brows drew together in confusion, and she frowned. "It's no fun having a boat if you just let it sit around moored all the time. I thought you loved sailing."

But I love you *more!* The remonstration came unbidden into his head, and nearly escaped past his lips. Eddie blinked in surprise at the unfamiliar inner voice that reared up so unexpectedly. Margot's look of puzzlement was slowly morphing into a glare as he sat with himself and introspected, but he couldn't pull his brain away from what it had just shouted at him.

He loved Margot. He wanted to keep Margot safe. If that much was true, and he was suddenly certain that it was, then that included keeping her safe from herself.

"I love sailing." He felt like a complete Neanderthal echoing what she had just said, and decided to try again. "But navigating the boat around here can be stressful, and we're supposed to be minimizing the stress in your life. Wouldn't you rather sit down and look over, uh…" What hadn't they done yet? "…nursery furniture with me? I'll turn the Wi-Fi back on."

"You're starting to sound like my mother," Margot said through her full-blown scowl. "I'll tell you what I told her, and it's that I have no interest in painting a room up in my apartment right now. Besides, we don't even know if the baby is a boy or a girl."

"You seemed pretty certain last week that it was a girl," Eddie pointed out quickly.

Margot shrugged. "It was just a hunch. It doesn't mean anything."

Now Eddie could feel his own temper starting to rise at this, and he quickly stamped it down. He didn't want to get in any sort of argument with Margot. Still...he had wondered before if she was being too flippant about this whole 'go with the flow thing', and had chalked it up as nothing more than a normal contrast to his own sudden, passionate need to take charge. But if she wasn't taking his concerns seriously, did that mean she wasn't taking other important matters – matters of her own *health* – at all seriously as well? He couldn't be there to watch her twenty-four-seven, no matter how hard he might try.

"Come on. It'll be fun," he said stiltedly. Eddie had no delusions of it being 'fun', but he needed to put on a brave face for Margot if she wasn't feeling it. "Go grab my laptop and I'll show you my Pinterest board."

"Really, Eddie? A Pinterest board?" She seemed willing enough to entertain him on this front, though, and disappeared below deck to grab his computer. He shouted down instructions to her on how to reconnect the Internet; by the time she resurfaced, he had steered the boat into a spot where he felt safe enough to idle while they spent some quality planning time together.

"See? We can go gender neutral, if you like," he mentioned as he clicked open his browser. "There's pastel yellows, greens...hell, we don't have to stick to any sort of heteronormative idea of what our baby colors should be."

Margot smiled as she settled in on one of the deck cushions beside him. "Such a way with words," she commended. Then: "I'm not worried about colors, Eddie. But you know most of this stuff won't fit inside my apartment."

"Of course," he agreed. He was eager to troubleshoot now that she had voiced a personal concern, and he was proud to have an easy answer for her. "All this will go in the classic six."

"What do you mean?" Margot stared at him, uncomprehending, and Eddie closed the laptop slowly.

"I meant to surprise you officially last night," he explained. "Margot, I bought the classic six for us to share. I thought maybe you suspected that's what I..." He cut himself off when he saw the look of horror that passed across her face. "Surprise," he concluded weakly.

"Eddie. You didn't."

There it was again: that flare in his chest, that feeling of wanting to get into an argument and knowing he had to suppress the urge. "Of course I did. I bought it for the three of us. Did you think I wouldn't plan for us to live together? Maybe the old Eddie wouldn't have—"

"I don't care about the old Eddie!" Margot exclaimed. She leapt to her feet with incredible agility for a boat-bound pregnant woman, and Eddie followed suit with a hand ready to stabilize her. She recoiled as if his touch was enough to sizzle her flesh; the way she wrenched her arm away from him was like a punch in the gut. "Did you think I would be happy to hear you made such a massive decision for us on your own? That you didn't even *think* to consult with me seriously about where I should live?"

"You should live with me, Margot!" Eddie exclaimed. "I didn't think it was that big a leap that you might want to live with your husband!"

And the man who loves you more than anyone. There was that voice again, that unfamiliar mental cadence that had appeared like a lightning bolt that morning and seemed insistent on stunning him again and again with the revelation that he had fallen for his childhood friend.

And there was said childhood friend, glaring at him like he had betrayed her worse than anyone to come before him by even attempting to put his money where his mouth is and provide for her and their child. Had he been wrong to purchase the apartment without her consent? He had thought Margot liked the classic six. But maybe this wasn't a matter of *like,* or *love.* It was a matter of something else...and it was something he had just fucked up royally.

"Turn the boat around," Margot said. "Please, Eddie. I need to get off now. I need to think." She pressed a hand to her forehead and turned away. He wanted nothing more in that moment than to go to her, to wrap her in his arms as he had the night before and physically enfold her.

Only he couldn't. He had tried to do everything right, and still somehow managed to push her away.

When Eddie looked at Margot now, he felt lost at sea.

CHAPTER ELEVEN

MARGOT

"That was a total dick move by Eddie," Trinity said. "Of course you freaked out and panicked. I definitely would have done the same." She slid the pastry plate toward Margot. "Here. You get full dibs today. I promise this will improve your mood."

Margot picked up her fork and toyed with the chocolate muffin, but her stomach was too busy doing flip-flops to signal her brain that she was truly hungry. She still wasn't sure why she had called Trinity about Eddie's apartment purchase. Margot knew Trinity kept busy with her work at the Jameson Agency, and had been surprised when Trinity isolated a block in her immediate schedule to devote to her. They had agreed to meet at a coffee shop near the firm Margot worked for – Trinity had been *very* enthusiastic about the muffin selection.

"So what's wrong with it?" Trinity asked as she sipped her coffee. "Does the view make it unlivable? Kitchen need to be completely redone? Did Eddie already section off a spot for his man cave?" She chuckled at her own mental image, and Margot couldn't blame her. It certainly seemed like something the old Eddie would do.

Trinity was a few years older than Margot, but they had been fast friends since their first meeting at a Jameson Agency Christmas party. Margot respected Trinity's judgement implicitly in all matters Eddie: she was maybe the only person who had learned to keep him in line over the years, and that was usually by just letting him be himself.

Margot shook her head in response. "That's the problem," she mumbled. "It's perfect. It's exactly as Eddie guessed: I *do* like it. I like everything about it."

Trinity fixed her with a measured look, and Margot quickly doubled-down on dismantling her muffin. She had the strangest intuition that Trinity had been fishing for an approval of the place, as if she had known Margot's true feelings all along. "So what's the problem?" Trinity inquired nonchalantly. "Aside from the obvious fact that Eddie went ahead without asking you. You guys can acknowledge that and move on, right?"

"I'm afraid it's symptomatic of how things are going to be." Margot sighed. "I don't want him making every important decision on his own. He may make them with me in mind, but he's still making them without me. I feel...left behind."

"You aren't being left behind," Trinity assured. "Eddie will come around. He's just freaking out a little bit right now. He wants so badly to show everyone what a responsible adult he is...and he wants to show you especially. He's just going about it in a slightly immature way." Trinity chuckled. "He thinks he can make a complete shift overnight, when the reality is he's making everyone around him, himself included, totally stressed out and miserable."

Margot's cheeks heated. "I don't want him to change himself because of me," she whispered. "And I *definitely* don't want him to change himself because of the baby. I agree he needed to learn some responsibility, but the Eddie I've always known...*that's* who I want to be the father of my child."

Trinity reached across the table and took the fork from Margot's hand. She gave her empty fingers a reassuring squeeze. "It sounds like you have to trust yourself on this one, Margot. You know how fond I am of Eddie—but is he right for you? At the end of the day, that's something only you can know. But it's something you have to consider, if the two of you have any chance of being happy—together or apart."

Margot's heart raced at Trinity's words. It was a silly reaction, she knew. It's not as if she needed to make a decision right here and now... but she realized her heart was beating so fast at the thought of *losing* Eddie. He may have gone about it in the densest way possible, but he had just gifted her with a dream apartment. Bigger than even the classic six was the gesture behind it: he was *thinking* of her. Looking out for her. Taking care of her. This wasn't a threat to her independence at all: it was an invitation by the man she loved to coexist as that same independent being alongside him.

"I love him," she blurted. She dropped her forehead into her free hand with a moan. "God, I don't know why it's so easy to tell you that, and not Eddie. I think that's why all this has got me so freaked out."

"It's finally becoming real," Trinity said. "Margot, if this is really what you want, then I can't express how happy I am for you. But you deserve to give all this as much thought as you need to. The two of you are making a big decision…"

"…and we're the only ones who can know if it's the right one," Margot finished for her.

Trinity nodded happily. Then she grinned. "Although, I don't mind being the deciding factor on another muffin. What do you say?"

"Of course I say yes," Margot said as they rose together. "I'm eating for two these days, remember?"

There was a knock at the door to the classic six.

Eddie stirred from where he lay stretched out on the couch. He massaged his forehead and blinked. "What time is it?" he muttered as he glanced around. He had managed to practically blanket himself in work papers and wedding receipts before dozing off. A glance out toward the patch of sky visible from the roof deck told him it was probably early evening; a rumble from his stomach told him he had already missed dinner.

He maneuvered himself into a seated position, blinked, yawned, and rose. He tapped his phone to check the time, and to see if he had received any texts from Margot while he was out, only to find it dead. She had been avoiding his attempts to contact her all week, and the entire wedding process had practically ground to a halt as a result. Not that Eddie couldn't handle all the planning himself, it was just that...

He found he didn't want to. When he had thought he was

taking work off Margot's plate, it had been different. Now, he felt like he was marrying a ghost rather than a prospective life partner. It was all too easy to feel unmotivated to prep the wedding now that he didn't even know if there was going to be a bride.

The knock at the door sounded again, rousing Eddie from his stupor. "Coming!" he called. He smoothed his rumpled hair and hopelessly stroked at the wrinkles in his shirt. He padded to the front door and pushed it open.

Margot stood on the mat, nervously trading her weight from one foot to the other. Eddie blinked. "Margie? I thought – " But what he thought didn't matter the next instant.

Margot rose up on her tiptoes to wrap her arms around his neck and kiss him full on the lips. Eddie grabbed her waist to affix her in place, letting his own lips roam over hers, until they shared a sigh of contentment and both drew back at the same time. He was so relieved to see her he felt like melting, and stopped just short of doing it when he remembered *he* was supposed to be the pillar of support in their relationship.

Still.

"It's so good to see you," he breathed. "I thought...I mean, I didn't think..."

"Shhh." Margot placed a gentle finger to his lips, and he clamped them shut obediently. They still felt kiss-starved, and even the most feather-light of her touches made him crave her mouth against his once more. "I wanted to apologize to you in person, Eddie. I'm sorry I reacted so negatively when you were trying to surprise me with such a wonderful gift. As much as I always thought I was ready to share my life with someone, the reality is that I never stopped to think about what that might *actu-*

ally mean. It means letting someone in, and inviting them to make important decisions that will affect you. It means trusting them." Margot shook her head. "I'm sorry I didn't see that."

"You really think the apartment's wonderful?" he asked hopefully. Margot drew her finger away and nodded. "Did I do good?"

"You did good." She smiled, and Eddie loved the way her adorable cheeks lifted. Any pregnancy weight she had managed to put on only made her look younger, and more beautiful; she looked well-rested and radiant today. "I didn't want to just come by and apologize," she added as she eased herself in against his chest. Her belly brushed his, and Eddie felt butterflies erupt within him. "I wanted to come by and thank you for taking so much on for us. *And* I wanted to invite you to go on a series of dates with me."

Eddie's eyebrows rose. "Really?"

Margot laughed and shook her head. "Well, I went ahead and booked us both for some classes on child care basics. I thought we could get some hands-on parenting training."

Eddie's heart fluttered. For a moment, he almost couldn't believe that this go-with-the-flow iteration of Margot was once again taking such an active interest in the preparation side of things. She was starting to act like her old self again, and he…

God, he was *relieved* to see her. This was a bad sign. The Eddie Margot needed most was the one who was responsible; who could assume control easily. She didn't need the boy who had always been relieved to let her handle things. He needed to be better than this; still, he couldn't resist letting his happiness at seeing the old Margot resurface go unvoiced.

"Is it gross that I find that impossibly romantic?" he asked her.

She laughed. "Absolutely!"

"Great. Want to double down on the evening's romance and order a pizza?" he inquired.

She raised an eyebrow. "I don't know. Is it on the recommended food list?"

"Screw the recommended food list," Eddie said as he slung his arm around her and steered her inside. "My child's going to learn to appreciate a good New York-style pizza from the womb."

Margot's laughter filled the apartment as the door swung shut behind him. For now, Eddie decided, it was the only furnishing he absolutely required to be happy.

The rest would come in due time.

CHAPTER TWELVE

EDDIE

W here are you?

Eddie stared down at the text from Margot. It was a week since what he had come to think of as the Forgiveness Pizza Party, and he had no idea what she was talking about. For a moment, he simply couldn't wrap his head around her question.

"Eddie?" Trinity asked him. "Is everything all right?"

Eddie glanced up. Sam and Trinity sat across from him at the conference room table. Sam had his finger poised above the conference call phone.

"Jonathan Daley's about to be on the other line," Sam mentioned. "He's going to know it if he doesn't have your full attention."

Eddie glanced back down at Margot's text. His head hurt; his vision blurred; and no matter how hard he squinted, he couldn't make her question ring out with any sense. He hadn't slept at all last night, and he had barely managed four hours the night before. He knew he was running on fumes, but there was no way he had missed anything in his schedule. She had probably texted the wrong person, or mistaken the day, or…

Then it hit him, as hard as if he had just rammed *Annabella* right into the dock. The fucking class! He had completely forgotten about the class Margot had signed them both up for, the one on parenting basics.

Eddie gripped the arms of his chair, heart hammering in his chest. He must have looked like a spooked animal about to bolt. Trinity's smile died, and her face, tan from living almost full-time in California, drained slightly of color. Sam watched and waited; then, when he clearly decided he couldn't wait anymore, he punched the button.

"Hello?" Jonathan Daley's voice came through the phone. "Eddie? You there?"

"I'm here." *But I should be somewhere else!* his mental voice shouted. *Where the hell am I supposed to be?*

"Trinity and I are here as well, Mr. Daley," Sam mentioned. His icy blue eyes were fixed on Eddie, but they were live now. Eddie didn't know how to convey to them that he had to go.

But he had to do something.

"Mr. Daley, I'm sorry, but I'm going to have to reschedule our meeting." It felt like someone else had taken hold and was speaking through his lips. "Something's come up."

"I beg your pardon?" Jonathan asked. "I set aside a whole two-hour block this morning to discuss your latest plans for my company's ad campaign, Eddie. If we want to launch next month, then time is of the essence. Isn't that what you told me?"

"Yes. I did tell you that." *Time is of the essence.* Eddie looked down at his phone. "But I think… I might have a personal emergency to attend to this morning."

"You *might?*" Jonathan's voice was cool and furious. "You better be sure of it, son. Because if you walk out of this meeting, then I might be forced to take my business to someone who knows how to prioritize with my best interests in mind."

Eddie wanted desperately to look to Trinity and Sam for backup. He wanted either, or both, of them to jump in and save him from having to make this decision. But if they could, they would have already done so. They were sitting at the same table, but Eddie was on his own.

"I do have your best interests in mind," he said quietly. "And that's why I have to go, Mr. Daley. It's Margot. She needs me."

"You've already shown your commitment to Margot. You're going to marry her like we agreed," Jonathan growled. Trinity's eyes bulged. She looked at Sam, but Sam looked just as surprised as she did by the news. Eddie closed his eyes against their incredulous faces, but he couldn't wince himself into nonexistence no matter how hard he tried. "Eddie? Do you hear me? She's my little girl, but whatever it is, it can wait."

"No. No, it can't wait. I'm sorry, Mr. Daley, but I have to go. I'm going to have to ask Sam and Trinity to take over this meeting for me." Eddie rose. "And if you need to reschedule, please talk to my secretary."

"Eddie, this had better be a fucking—"

Sam muted the call and turned to Eddie. "You're really taking off?"

"I have to," Eddie said. "I'm sorry to you both, but… Margot. I have to find Margot." He knew he was rattling on, that he wasn't making any sense, but her name was the ticket he needed to get out of the room. He sprinted down the hallway, thumbing open his schedule as he rushed for the next elevator. Why hadn't his reminder popped up? Had he even remembered to set one?

On my way, he texted Margot in the elevator. Then he leaned back against the wall and shut his eyes.

His ride through the city was a complete blur. By the time he arrived at the building across town hosting the class, he was exhausted. He had forgotten how many cups of coffee he'd had already to keep going. Had he had any espresso since yesterday evening at dinner?

"Fuck," Eddie whispered below his breath. The cab halted, and he piled out of the back. He hadn't had the time to wait for someone to bring his car around back at the agency. Margot was sitting alone on the stone steps leading up to the building's front entrance. When her eyes lifted, and she saw Eddie, she grabbed the railing and hauled herself unsteadily to her feet.

Too late, Eddie thought desperately. *I'm always too late for everything that counts. I try to get out ahead of everything...I try to be the man she needs, and I...*

"Where were you?" Margot's eyes were black as storm clouds. Eddie froze. He wanted to take a step back, but that would have put him back out in the flow of heavy traffic.

Then again, maybe that would have been the best decision he made all day.

"Margot. I am *so* sorry," he emphasized.

"The class is over. I did it all alone." There were tears in her voice, and crystalline beads trembling in the corners of her eyes, even though her words were dreadfully steady. "I was the only person there by myself."

"God, Margot. I am sorry." Just looking at her he could feel his heart breaking. "How can I make it up to you? Just name it. I'll do anything."

Margot shook her head. Eddie had the impression that she wasn't even listening to him, not really; those shimmering storm cloud eyes were distant now, as if the danger of a downpour had already passed him by. "I want to be the best parent possible to our child, Eddie. I *want* to get married. I *want* to move into the classic six. I want to be involved in every part of her – or his – life. I want to be like my parents were with me."

"Involved," Eddie repeated.

Margot glanced up from the familial fantasy she was entertaining; her eyes refocused on him, curious about something she sensed in his tone. "I'm sorry?"

"Your parents are so involved in everything, Margot. More than you can know."

"What do you mean by that?" she asked. "Eddie?"

"I mean that it was your father's idea all along that I ask you to marry me." The words, the truth, bled past his lips before he could think to stop them up. He was so tired he wasn't thinking straight. Was this the right time? Was there any right time to tell her? He couldn't gauge anymore. All he could do was latch onto what she was saying, and hope his instincts weren't steering him completely untrue.

He needed to say more, though, because now Margot was staring at him as if he had grown a second head...and as if that head looked very much like her own father. "But I...I asked because I love you, Margot," he said in a rush. "I didn't want to tell you like this...I didn't want to tell you *any* of this." He raked a hand through his hair. "But I love you. I know that much. Even if I'm making up the rest as I go."

"Love me?" she repeated. She sounded faint. Eddie reached for her, to help her sit back down if need be, and she shook him off her elbow. "How can you...Eddie, my father...were the two of you just troubleshooting a *scandal?* Was that what this was all along?" The tears sprang into her eyes again. "Is that all I am to you? How can you say you love me *and* that this was all my father's idea in practically the same sentence?"

"Margot, wait—"

"No, Eddie. I'm *done* waiting. I've been waiting all along for you to figure out what kind of man you want to be. It just...this isn't working. I wanted it to. God, I wanted it to." Margot straightened her shoulders and glared past him, as if she could direct her disproval inward and vaporize whatever weakness she saw there. "But I've never been someone who needed to be looked after. No matter what you *or* my father might think. I can attend parenting classes on my own. I *can* take care of myself without you."

"Margot—"

But she brushed by him without another word and disappeared resolutely down the street. Eddie could do nothing but watch her go.

CHAPTER THIRTEEN

EDDIE

"Margot...girl...*what* are you doing?" Margot muttered below her breath as she let herself in through the dock's security gate.

It was the question of the century, and one Margot had been posing to herself more and more often over the course of the last several months. 'Going with the flow' of things was proving to be easier said than done. She had always imagined the 'flow' as being something relaxing, something that would move along at a leisurely pace and work itself out in the end regardless of any force of will she tried to exercise over it. What she hadn't imagined was for her 'flow' to take the form of an unstoppable tidal wave that she couldn't prevent from crashing down around her, again and again and again. She felt like a perpetual Coney Island tourist at the beach with only a pool floaty to protect her.

She laid a hand on her stomach, as she often did now, and felt a sudden rush of comfort. She walked down along the dock, and she barely noticed the way it occasionally pitched gently beneath her feet. Eddie's boat rose up out of the fading light, proud and safe and familiar. She was here at his invitation.

She was here because she wanted a future together with him.

It was something Margot had found difficult to accept at first...even more difficult than the reality of her pregnancy, and of a potential marriage to the man who was her best friend. She had loved him for longer than she could possibly know. It was such a frightening revelation that all she had wanted to do at first was run from Eddie, and from the tangled web he had managed to weave around them in the name of doing the right thing.

No, it wasn't the perfect fantasy. But maybe it was better than that. They were a *family*. A dysfunctional, expectant family, but a family nonetheless, and their potential was limitless. When she thought about their relationship in those terms, the web suddenly disappeared, and was replaced by strings of attachment that could never be severed.

She loved Eddie. He, and the baby, and her happiness, trumped everything else. She was ready to take this plunge into the unknown with him. Nothing needed to be perfectly mapped out ahead of time... but that also didn't mean she needed to sit back and let fate take the wheel. She would be actively participating in this, because something told her it would be the most worthwhile thing she would ever do. And she wasn't willing to leave that to chance; to *flow*. Anything she cared about this much required her complete involvement, from beginning to end. She saw that clearly now.

She arrived at the boat; when she noticed the shadow of movement onboard, she glanced up from trying to navigate the step stool. Eddie was there, waiting for her. He cleared his throat, before bending to hold out a hand to her. Margot accepted without thinking and boarded.

"Evening, Margot," he said. "I'm glad you got my text."

"Evening, Eddie," she said. "I'm glad you decided to text me."

He was dressed up in his most formal yachting attire, looking as effortless as he did immaculate. His auburn hair was brushed back, though not slicked down; he was clean-shaven, but still wore the faint shadow of stubble that she had grown to love. It starkly differentiated the man from the boy she had once known. Margot's heart did a somersault now to see him standing in the faint light of the cabin, and kept up its sudden circus audition when she noticed the way he was looking at her. His eyes glimmered with an emotional sheen, like he still didn't quite trust his vision every time he looked at her.

He didn't let go of her hand.

"Margot, thank you for coming," he said. "I wanted the chance to explain everything to you. I wanted you to know that it's true when I first proposed to you, I did it because your father asked me to."

"I really doubt he 'asked'," Margot said, with a twist of a smile to let him know it was all right to go on.

Eddie chuckled. "If it had been up to me, I would have waited until I felt the time was right. I would have waited until we had discussed everything first, rather than try to play catch-up alongside making such a rash decision. But... I gave that responsibility to someone else. I let your father lead. And I know now that your father has no place in our relationship. Nobody does. And I may not always know how to do the right thing, but I'm

the one who has to own my decisions. I can't outsource them."
He looked at her a long moment. "I might have lost us your dad's
account. And that's okay. I intend to win him back one day... *and*
to win his approval. But I'm not going to go looking for it. And
I'm not going to let it be the thing that motivates me to be a good
husband to you."

"Oh, Eddie." Margot's heart broke to hear him say it, but she
also couldn't deny the flood of relief she felt.

"I know now that the partnership that's most important to me
requires me to learn to split responsibility and act as part of a
team. This is your life, Margot, as much as it's mine. We're inter-
twined now."

Eddie's hand, the one that didn't hold hers, found her stomach. He touched the exact same spot that Margot had touched
earlier, his hand filling the invisible handprint she had left
behind. Tears sprang into the corners of her eyes.

"When I tried to exercise control over everything, it all went
to shit," he remarked. Margot let out an outburst of laughter, the
sound tinged with the emotion she was trying so hard to
suppress, and Eddie's accompanying laugh was equally raw and
relieved. "But I'm done trying to be so clinical and formal and
aggravatingly *right* about everything. I want the life we were
meant to have, if I wasn't trying so hard to be someone I'm not."

"Thank God," Margot said. She squeezed his hand in hers.

"Thank you, Margot," Eddie emphasized. "Thank you for
being yourself. Thank you for standing by me and being the
woman I could look at all along and realize I loved. Just knowing
that now makes every fuck-up worth it to me. I'm just sorry it
was such a journey for us both."

"I love you too, Eddie Jameson," she said. She stood before him, with only their child between them, and she knew her eyes shone as brightly as his own as she declared the truth to him. "I still want to marry you. More than anything, I want to marry you." She gave another half-laugh, half-sob, and felt such relief in the aftermath of telling him. "I want to spend the rest of my life with you."

"Then I don't want to let another minute pass us by," he said. "Do you?"

Margot shook her head. "There's the impulsive Eddie I love. Not even another second more, if I could help it," she agreed.

Eddie grinned. "I'm glad you said it." He turned, and whistled over his shoulder. Margot rose up on her tiptoes to watch, as two shadows she hadn't noticed before moved out from the wheelhouse.

"Sam!" she exclaimed in surprise. "Trinity! What are you doing here?"

Eddie's brother and his partner materialized out of the shadows. Sam was dressed well, as always, although his attire was definitely unsuitable to boating; Trinity looked graceful and lovely in a breezy taupe dress unlike anything Margot had ever seen her wear before. She had only ever known Trinity to dress conservatively for the office, or slightly more expensively for work functions.

"My brother Sam is newly ordained," Eddie explained.

"We set it up online, but it still counts. I ran it past Legal." Sam spoke stiffly, and Margot realized he looked like the most nervous one present. "But if the two of you are ready to get started, shall we?"

"I'm here as a witness," Trinity confided. She took Margot's arm affectionately in her own and squeezed. "We promised Eddie we'd jump ship as soon as the two of you are husband and wife."

"I can't believe it." Margot was almost too choked for words as she looked between the three of them, but she couldn't keep her eyes off Eddie for long, even if she tried. "I don't think you understand. I've dreamed about this for so long. Is this really happening?"

Eddie held his hand out for her, his smile beaming from ear to ear. "What do you say, Margot? Want to get hitched? Want to have your dream wedding right here, right now?"

Margot stepped forward. She placed her hand in Eddie's own, enjoying the last time she would ever come into contact with her fiancé. "I do."

She couldn't wait until the hand she held was her husband's.

EPILOGUE

Margot entered the kitchen of the Classic Six at seven A.M. Sunday morning. She crossed, bleary-eyed, to the espresso machine, completely ignoring anything else. She was a woman on a mission.

Eddie was already seated at the table, holding their baby girl in his arms.

"Good morning, Margie," he greeted amicably. Margot grunted something that might have been assent, or it might have been profanity – Eddie wasn't completely versed in her pre-coffee dialect – and punched the button on the machine. She had done it enough times without loading up the coffee first that Eddie had taken to getting ahead of her schedule: he always kept the shots preloaded now. It had taken discovering her sipping a cup of hot water, too tired to notice the lack of caffeine, for him to realize an intervention might be in order.

Margot didn't like to be reminded of that episode.

She'd been up three times already that night tending to the baby. Eddie could tell she was feeling the weariness down to her bones, but she still somehow managed to look completely radiant. No makeup, no hair product, no cutting-edge designer dress. It was just Margot, his wife, standing in a shaft of sunlight in the apartment they shared, naturally luminous – and tantalizingly curvaceous – in the sheer nightgown he had bought for her. She glanced sidelong and caught him looking, but Eddie didn't avert his eyes. No matter what exhausted mood she might be in, he wanted her to know that he couldn't help looking when she entered the room. When he smiled, she smiled back.

But she didn't hold his undivided attention for long. Their daughter gave a small, gasping choke, and stretched her limbs. Eddie's eyes dropped, and he rocked her in his arms, murmuring nonsense words until she quieted and fell back asleep. When he looked to Margot again, he saw his wife's eyes shimmering.

"How's our Annabella?" she asked.

"Great. Beautiful. Extraordinary. Like her mother." Eddie rocked the tiny bundle in his arms. "Why do you ask?"

"Because she hasn't made a peep since you picked her up and brought her out here," Margot said in a tone of fond exasperation.

"What can I say? She's Daddy's girl already." He grinned.

"Is that a bet you're willing to take?" Margot asked. "Because I'd say it's game on, Daddy. I'm going to buy her absolutely everything her little heart desires when your back is turned."

"We're going to spoil her like hell," Eddie noted.

"You better believe it." Margot turned away momentarily to

doctor her espresso. Eddie watched the elegant movement of her wrist as she stirred in the cream; he observed the minute way her body swayed in place. Meeting his daughter had only made him love the woman who gave birth to her all the more. He had never imagined he would find such utter euphoric happiness, especially not at seven in the morning after sharing another sleepless night with the two members of his new family.

He was going to get emotional if he kept thinking this way. He had better turn his attention to something else.

"Hey, so what's this package about?" Eddie nodded to the unopened box on the table. "Did you order something?" It nagged at him a little to think he hadn't anticipated something Margot might need, but he was more curious than anything.

"Oh, I don't know." Margot's eyes were evasive. *Suspiciously* evasive. "Why don't you open it?"

"I'll see if I can manage," Eddie chuckled. "But if I wake our daughter, it's on you."

"Deal," Margot said. She turned back to doctor her coffee as Eddie dragged the package toward him.

"So what is it?"

"I took a page out of your book. I hope you don't mind." Margot alighted on the kitchen chair across from him, mug in hand. Her eyes, beautiful above the temporary lines of exhaustion that creased her face, were focused intently on him. He knew something was up, but he was willing to string the game along for a few moments longer.

"Really?" Eddie raised the package to his ear and gave it a little shake. He was stalling for time while he tried to guess its contents. "How so?"

Margot shrugged one thin shoulder. "I just wanted to take something off your plate," she explained. "You've taken charge of so much for us." She reached across the table to wiggle one of Annabella's exposed toes. "Didn't he?" she crooned. "Anyway, I remember that it was always such a relief to see that you'd thought of something when I was too preoccupied to even see straight. Sooo I thought I'd surprise you."

"A surprise?" Eddie repeated. Normally he would have had some idea of what was coming, but this morning he found himself at a complete loss. Maybe Margot wasn't the only one who needed espresso to resume normal brain function. As if reading his mind, Margot rose to refill his own coffee mug as Eddie tore into the delivery one-handed.

"Baby announcements," he marveled as soon as he had cleared the packaging away. "Margot, I completely forgot about even ordering these."

"I know." Margot grinned. "What do you think of my design?"

"You did these yourself?" Eddie fanned a hand along the announcements. The more intently he looked, the more he thought he could identify Margot's artistic stamp, and the touch that made her such a highly sought-after architect: the announcements were elegant and utilitarian, the words traced in soft silvers and grays on raised type. They were as gorgeous to look at as they were to feel, and they were completely unlike any birth announcements Eddie had ever personally received. "No powderpuff pink?" he joked. Of course Margot would forgo what would be expected.

"Look closer," she encouraged.

Eddie drew Annabella in against his chest and leaned in to read the announcement. His sleep-deprived brain had glossed over everything except the name of their daughter; now, he saw the full message.

Mr. and Mrs. Jameson would like to invite you to join them in welcoming baby Annabella into the world.

"Mister and Misses..." He still couldn't comprehend what he was reading. "Margot, did you mean to...?"

"Announce our marriage alongside the birth?" Margot came around the table with his coffee, and Eddie shifted Annabella so that his wife could seat herself on his thigh. She set his mug down and kissed his cheek. "Of course I did."

"I..." Eddie was choked for words. He glanced between his child and the woman he loved, and couldn't think of what he was meant to say – *he,* Eddie Jameson, semi-famous ad exec and formerly notorious party boy. The guy who could talk his way into, and out of, anything, had expended every word that might possibly describe how he was feeling in that moment.

Margot giggled, and swooped in to plant another quick kiss. "You should see your face right now," she murmured. "It's so cute. Almost as cute as our daughter."

Eddie's eyes burned with emotion. When Margot tried to steal another peck, he leaned in and captured her lips with his own. She sighed against his mouth and leaned in, threading her arms around the back of his neck. "I love you, Mrs. Jameson," he murmured.

"I love you, Mr. Jameson," she returned.

Between them, the biggest surprise of all – the one who had arrived unexpectedly, and brought their beautiful family together – slept on.

END OF THE BILLIONAIRE'S PREGNANT FLING

JAMESON BROTHERS BOOK TWO

PS: Do you like novels that are hot, heavy and free? Keep reading for an exclusive extract from the Greek Billionaire's Blackmailed Bride.

THANK YOU!

Thank you so much for purchasing my book. It's hard for me to put into words how much I appreciate my readers. If you enjoyed this book, please remember to leave a review. Reviews are crucial for an author's success and I would greatly appreciate it if you took the time to review the book. I love hearing from you!

If you enjoyed this book please leave a review at:
LeslieNorthBooks.com

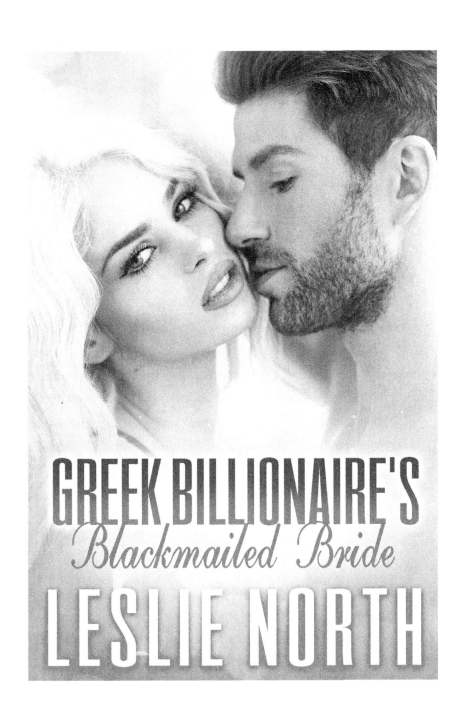

GREEK BILLIONAIRE'S
Blackmailed Bride
LESLIE NORTH

BLURB

Greek banking heir Antonio Rosso is shocked when his late father leaves the beloved family villa to the one woman he never wanted to see again: Claire Bennett.

After a hot and heavy fling, things ended abruptly when she was accused of being a gold digger. But now, to hang on to the home that meant so much to his mother, Antonio will not only have to get back into the beautiful American's good graces, he'll have to convince her to marry him.

When a job brings her back to Greece, voiceover artist Claire should have guessed Antonio was behind it. With his entitled upbringing, she knows he's learned to use his money to get his way. After the way she was treated though, she wants absolutely nothing to do with him. He may be even more sinfully handsome than she remembered, but if he thinks she'll agree to a sham marriage, he has another thing coming.

Claire is determined to prove she can't be bought or sold, and Antonio needs nothing more than a temporary arrangement. But when their spark reignites, can they ever get past the ugly history between them?

Grab your FREE COPY of the Greek Billionaire's Blackmailed Bride at www.LeslieNorthBooks.com

EXCERPT

It was almost too bad Petrakis hadn't died instead.

Antonio Rosso listened to the man drone on…and on. He knew Petrakis had never approved of him, but the lawyer seemed to be taking pleasure in detailing every bequest in the will—every small donation, every tiny remembrance, every charity that would get part of his father's vast estate.

Or had this been his father's idea? Matthias Rosso had been a despot in life—and in death he still wanted everyone to dance to the tune he set. Antonio shifted on his feet, and got a glare from his sister, Alexandra.

Both his sisters had straight, black hair—like his mother had. They also had the same dark eyes. An old familiar pain twisted inside Antonio—regret his mother had not lived, the ache of memory, the wish just to see her once more. But he did see her—he could see her any time he looked at his sisters. He wished that was comfort enough, but he would have to make do with no more arguments with his father.

Alexandra gave him one more glare that told him to behave. Even though Antonio was the eldest, Alexandra had become their mother after Livia Rosso had died. She sat next to Eva now, holding Eva's hand, while Antonio stood, leaning on a bookcase filled with musty, leather-clad legal volumes. At least Antonio assumed they were legal books. His mouth twitched at the thought of opening one and finding a Playboy centerfold.

Petrakis raised an eyebrow and cleared his throat. Antonio tried to pay more attention. Did Petrakis think he was telling them anything new? Matthias had already told them most of this time and time again, usually with the stipulation that if they did not behave they would get nothing.

Antonio listened to the list of residences scattered around Europe and even in North America—his father's hobby, he thought, collecting places as well as people, and money that could have been better spent.

Finally Petrakis got to the family.

"To my daughters Alexandra and Eva, I leave each a trust fund of fifty-million US dollars to be administered by their older brother Antonio until each of my daughters reaches the age of twenty-five. If either of my daughters should marry before the age of twenty-five, I leave it up to my son to release the trust or to continue to manage it." Antonio straightened, anger tightening his jaw and stomach. Petrakis glanced at him. "Your father included that condition because he didn't want his daughters to be targets for men who would marry for money only. It is your decision as to whether any man is to be entrusted with such a large sum of money."

Antonio snorted. "As if they aren't smart enough to know that. My father thought we lived in the eighteen hundreds, when women couldn't be trusted with anything." He glanced at his sisters. Alexandra sat still, her dark eyes flat, but color burned in her cheeks. Eva kept her head down. Antonio would have to talk to them later. They could break this trust—or he would simply put them in charge of their own money.

Petrakis shook his head and began to read again. "To my son, Antonio, I leave this world with a heavy heart for the wrongs I have done. There was a time when Antonio found it easy to trust others. But that changed, and I blame myself for that. To make up for this, I leave the rest of my estate to my son, with the exception of the Villa Livia on Kato Antikeri, which goes to Claire Bennett."

Antonio straightened. His sisters did as well and Eva asked, "Claire who?" She looked at Antonio, but he did not remove his stare from Petrakis. The lawyer put down the will and folded his hands on top of it.

Crossing his arms, Antonio asked, "Tell me what it's going to take to break this will. I am not allowing my mother's house— the place where she is buried, the villa named after her, to go to…to an American."

"You know this Claire?" Alexandra asked.

Antonio ignored her question as well.

Petrakis lifted an eyebrow. "There is one more condition." He cleared his throat and read, "Everything will be held in trust for my son until he is married. At that time he may do as he pleases, and if he marries by his twenty-fifth birthday, the rest of my inheritance, including the Villa Livia, will go to him."

Alexandra gave a gasp. "That's next month! That's crazy!"

Petrakis put a hand on the document. "Your father was of sound mind. The bequests are all reasonable, if a touch…unusual."

Grab your FREE COPY of the Greek Billionaire's Blackmailed Bride from www.LeslieNorthBooks.com

Printed in Great Britain
by Amazon

35791828R00086